1

The Temple Of The Blue Dog

By

R.J. Harris

Published by Dog Star Publications,

Printed by Lulu.com 2014.

The Temple Of The Blue Dog.

ISBN 9780473336660

Copyright © R.J.Harris, 2014.

The author welcomes any comments and can be contacted using the following email address: **drzargle1@gmail.com**

Prologue:

Today in many west European societies there is a growing sense of panic, of some ill-defined feeling of conflict. This sense of foreboding is really the acute dissonance between the traditional ideals of western liberalism and the more militant demands of a strident religious dogma. My story **'The Temple Of The Blue Dog'** *is set at some unspecified future date when a new, highly misogynistic religion has become the dominant, legal force in society.*

The narrative consists of two stories which run consecutively. One involves a father from the caste of Untouchables who is desperately seeking medical help for his gifted daughter Rosie. The other story is about Susan, an open-minded young woman who decides to leave her city but who slowly becomes ensnared by the new restrictions imposed on females. Both stories run in alternating sections of about two pages each, eventually merging into a single narrative in the closing pages as Rosie and her father intersect with Susan's life.

The Temple Of The Blue Dog

'Daddy, I saw those sparks again last night.'

'Oh Rosie darlin', you've been havin' dreams again that's all. Have y'breakfast it'll make y'feel better.' Rosie's father replied softly.

Waving away some flies, he pushed a broken, wooden board across the floor towards Rosie. On it were some slices of limp cabbage leaves and a few brown chunks of apple.

Of all his five children Rosie's father was most in love with Rosie. When he looked at her, he often felt a pain so deep inside it was hard for him not to cry. The reason, he knew, was that Rosie was somehow 'different' from the other kids. She was 'special' in a way he didn't really understand. Sometimes he could sense it in the way Rosie looked at things and, sometimes, he could even see it.

He first noticed something about a year ago, maybe six or seven winters after she was born. He found her on the pile, sitting down and staring intently at some wet papers that had been bent and twisted by the bulldozers. She was carefully unpicking the stuck-together pages and her eyes were following the rows of black marks. None of his other children had ever behaved like this – they just did as they were told: tear open the bags, get out the metal, hard plastics and glass – but Rosie, he noticed, often sat there, completely still and appeared 'lost' as though dreaming with her eyes wide open. She was either looking straight ahead at nothing or staring down at those rows and rows of black marks.

'They're comin'!! They're comin'!!!' someone shouted outside the plastic shelter.

Like an explosion of excitement Rosie's brothers and sisters all ran out into the sunshine.

'There he is!' one of the eldest called out pointing at something in the distance. Immediately all the children ran like crazy things towards a tiny dot of blue zigzagging its way across the multi-coloured pile of bags. All the children but one.

'Come, let's go see,' said Rosie's father taking her hand.

'You know what they want don't you?' commented Rosie's mother as she left the tent and stood up straightening her back. Rosie was old enough to know that inside her mother's big round tummy was another baby brother or sister and that she herself had come from the very same place. How she had got to be inside her mother was a question that often left Rosie puzzled but very determined to understand.

'Don't worry mother, I've got something saved for them.' Rosie's father replied over his shoulder as he and Rosie walked from the tent.

More parents from other tents were now standing and watching as their children raced across the mountains of bags to greet the little Blue Dog.

The children knew, of course, they were not allowed to touch the Blue Dog, but they also knew it was a blessing if the Blue Dog came and sniffed them or even better licked their hand – that, they were told, was a sign they had been chosen by the ancestors. Then, not far behind the Blue Dog, came the priests. There were about six of them all walking in a line. Around their waists they wore a broad sash of some stunning blue-gold material, while wrapped around their heads was a band of the same blue and gold. Though nobody understood what they meant, even at this distance you could hear them chanting the same words over and over –

'Malus spicatum et nostrum verdammt! Malus spicatum et nostrum verdammt!'

The dog itself was indeed a friendly creature whose long, fluffy fur had been completely dyed an iridescent blue – it almost seemed to shine blueness. But, like every dog, it was only really interested in smells – which is why it had followed its nose to the city dump. However, the followers, the acolytes, the priests and devotees of the Blue Dog worshiped the animal because they believed it symbolised the Sanctity of Chaos, the unpredictable expression of the Divine Spirit they said – or was it the divine spirit of Unpredictable Expression? Some priests called it the Catholicism of Chaos – which became known as the 'Chaothic Way'. But, from the words they spoke, it was sometimes hard to tell what they were talking about. Nevertheless, Chaos seemed to play a big part in their thinking, and as a result, whichever way the dog went – following the random odours that swept by its nose – the priests also went. The Blue Dog's 'chaothic' path was, they insisted, the only path to the true God.

The crowd of ragged children formed a wide, respectful circle around the little Blue Dog and watched as it methodically smelt each bag of rubbish and finally chose the most promising. Then wagging its tail with great excitement it used its two front paws and began ripping open a bag and tucking in to some left-over chicken bones. When it had finished eating it started to slowly walk around in circles, then stopped and dropped a small pile of excrement on one of the bags.

Immediately the blue-robed priests went down on their knees and instructed the circle of children to do the same. The priests lifted up their hands, palms outwards and began to sing in some incomprehensible monotone – the Hymn to Blue Excrement they called it. Then one of the devotees at the rear came forward with what looked like a gold casket and a tiny silver shovel. He went over to the Blue Dog's offering, scooped it up and placed it in the casket. The casket was then ceremoniously sealed with a blue ribbon and placed in yet another casket – this time one covered with jewels that sparkled in the sunlight. By now, however, the Blue Dog had moved on and the sacred Chaothic Path to God called yet again, and so the priests rose and, together with the excited children, followed the animal down towards the village of plastic tents.

*

'A celebrity's tits! – boring! Microwaved kittens! – boring! Fried foetus and chips! – boring! Sex with dolphins! – boring! It's all been done! You'd better come up with something new! Something fresh! Viewers want something to make them vomit and shit their pants all at the same time! Find it!' the editor shouted as he left slamming the office door.

Susan sat with her eyes closed imagining herself pushing the editor into a swimming pool full of hungry sharks. She hated her boss so much – this fat, red-faced bully with bad breath and a bad mind – and she hated her job – a reporter for an online news channel. But at twenty three she knew she was exceptionally lucky to have work – there were far too many, more qualified than her, who at thirty three still hadn't found a job and probably never would.

She got up and went over to the mirror, arranged her blue mask and left her office. She went down the stairs and out into the busy street. The predominant colour outside was also blue. All females, without exception, had to wear a blue mask in public – the *jiba* it was called. Ever since the Restoration of Morality Act had been passed, it was now mandatory for women to follow the dress code as defined by 'Ordinance 112: The Rectification of Correct Feminine Modesty'. The consequences of not wearing the jiba were just too horrible to contemplate – there were Morality Guardians (or MG's) – on almost every street corner. They wore dark blue uniforms, filmed everyone who went passed and they were armed. You didn't argue with them. They were mostly men, of course, but sometimes they were women – and it was the women Morality Guardians who were the most cruel.

Susan walked down several streets and entered a cafe where she often had lunch. She ordered a coffee and sat down to think. Naturally, she was not allowed to remove her jiba in public, even in a cafe, which made drinking her coffee a delicate process. But like most things she had found a way and grown used to it – she lifted the bottom of the jiba up with one hand and brought the edge of the cup to her lips with the other – simple really.

The cafe door opened and another masked women entered and, although the cafe had plenty of empty tables, she deliberately came and sat down opposite Susan at her table. Susan looked at the woman's eyes – they were dark and looking intently at Susan's. No one spoke. Then slowly the other woman slid her hand across the table, gently took Susan's hand and said softly,

'Hello.'

Alarmed, Susan quickly stood up, drained her coffee, and left the cafe. She walked with her head down, rapidly turning corner after corner only now and again glancing behind to make sure she wasn't being followed. Susan had heard of these people but this was the first time it had happened to her. One of the things the Restoration of Morality Act had allowed was the establishment of a Moral Entrapment Force – 'gay busters' they had once been called years ago, before the word 'gay' had been declared morally illegal and expunged from the dictionary. Their sole job was to find those in the community whom they suspected were sexually deviant – and to denounce them. And once a person had been denounced – whether rightly or wrongly – their life, as they had known it, was over.

Susan came to a small park and wanted desperately to go and sit down in the sunshine to get her breath back and to quietly think and calm her mind. But women were not allowed in parks alone – they had to be in the company of either their husbands or a male relative. She clenched her fists with anger, turned around and walked down several more streets not caring where she was going.

Then, in a crazy bid to feel she was escaping, Susan noticed a bus stop across the road. She decided to cross over and catch a bus – any bus would do as long as it moved away from here, away from this insane world. But then, in the distance, she noticed only the blue, male-only buses coming her way. There wasn't a single green, female-only bus in sight. Feeling her anger beginning to turn into rage Susan looked around, and – fortunately – further down the street she spotted a small local library. With a feeling of relief she quickly walked on and went through the library doors. Without even glancing at its title, Susan chose a book from one of the shelves and found a quiet corner. She sat down in an armchair and closed her eyes and tried to think. Fuck the editor! Fuck her job! Fuck the Morality Laws! Fuck the park and buses! Fuck them! Fuck them all! She wanted out! She wasn't going back!

*

'....and although worms will destroy your body, yet in your flesh shall you see the Blue Dog....'

Inside one of the larger plastic tents, six blue priests sat in a wide semicircle almost surrounding several dozen ragged children. The little Blue Dog the children had run to welcome, now lay sleeping at one of the priest's feet.

'Every time you do something wrong a part of you – deep inside here,' the priest slapped his chest loudly making the children jump, 'a part of you turns into a six-headed cockroach that begins to eat its way out of your body...' the priest finished. Then another added,

'But every time you do something good, a golden feather is added to the wings you will be given when you enter heaven...' he said.

Each time one of the priests spoke within the semicircle, the children's heads turned towards the voice, their eyes wide, their minds completely spellbound with awe and fear.

'And even thinking wrong, wicked thoughts can make your brain slowly turn into a poisonous, green custard that drips from your ears...' Here the priest paused, looked at the children's terrified faces and finished,

'So you must always be true to the Blue Dog.'

'And then there are the Devs!' another priest suddenly shouted.

'Ahhh!! We forgot to mention the Devs!!' another dramatically echoed.

'The Devs are the foulest, meanest demons ever created! They haunt your hands! They shriek inside your heads! They infest your eyes and spread the stench of human filth inside your mouths! But!...But worst of all – they breed between your legs! They make you hot and eager to play with them! Crazed with carnal desire they scream at you in the night 'Touch me! Touch me!' until you are reduced to a mass of fornicating jelly!'

'But... ,' another priest whispered passionately, 'Our Blue Dog (peace be with it) is the enemy of the Devs! He is your Eternal Saviour! And why? – because he loves you of course! One day you will ride on his back as he takes you through the jewelled gates of heaven! He is your protector! Here, here – take these,' the priest opened a bag next to him and brought out several handfuls of necklaces each with a small plastic pendent of their Eternal Saviour. Soon every child was wearing a glowing Blue Dog around their neck.

'Remember, always wear these to help protect you from the Devs. The Blue Dog will keep you safe!'

One of the children raised a small arm. The priests looked at each other a little unsure and then one asked the child,

'Yes, what is it?'

'Do Blue Dogs grow old?' Rosie's tiny voice asked.

'Err yes...yes I suppose they do...why do you ask child?'

'If they grow old, then someday do they die?'

'Well..' the priest answered trying to be light-hearted, 'Well, I suppose, our little friend here – ' and he patted the Blue Dog still sleeping at his feet, 'will one day run into heaven wagging his tail and meet his glorious maker.'

'So if they die and go to heaven, then they can't be here to protect us?'

'How dare you child! Question us like this!' one of the priests growled and for emphasis he stood up and tried to tower like a giant over the children.

'If...' he grumbled loudly, 'you are tempted to scorn the Blue Dog, your name child,' and here he pointed directly at Rosie, 'will go down into the book of those who have never existed!'

'But that's silly,' Rosie replied quietly without any hint that she was intimidated by the priest and his pompous words. The priest's face started to go rather red but before he could release his anger Rosie continued, 'Because if you put someone's name in a book, it shows they did exist.'

'This child is haunted! Go! Go!' All the priests stood up and within seconds the children had scattered.

'Where is the child's father!?' one of the priests demanded.

'She is my child sir – I am sorry,' Rosie's father said as he came forward from the entrance of the tent.

'Her mouth is haunted. She uses sinning words! You must beat her! And it is time she wore her jiba! She displays too much flesh! You must cover her arms and especially her legs.'

'Yes! Before they begin breeding!' another priest hissed.

'Yes sir. She is young, please forgive her.' Rosie's father replied and he handed over to one of the priests a small pouch of money. The priest opened the pouch and looked up at Rosie's father saying,

'Is this all?'

'It's been a bad month sir. In all the years we've lived here the price of scrap has never been lower.'

The priest showed the open pouch to some of the others.

'With this the gates of heaven will be forever closed!' one of them hissed.

'I do, sir, have something a bit...a bit special, if you would like?'

'Special? What?'

'It's a bottle we found in one of the bags – I've been saving it for your honours.' Rosie's father replied.

'A bottle? What's in it?'

'A dark, brown liquid sir.'

'Have you opened it?'

'No sir, I've kept it for your honours.'

'Well let's see it.'

Rosie's father went to a dark corner of the shelter and returned holding a large slim bottle.

'There's no label?' a priest queried.

'No sir. It must be very, very old. The label has washed off – and anyway, I wouldn't have been able to read it.'

'It's on the glass daddy.' Rosie said standing at the entrance to the shelter.

All the priests turned.

'It's her!' one of them muttered, 'The child with the haunted mouth!'

'I am not haunted.' Rosie corrected, totally unmoved by their comments, and she continued, 'The glass has raised letters – you can feel them and see them. Look, I'll show you.' Rosie walked boldly into the group of priests who all stepped back as though afraid of her.

Rosie took the bottle and, running her fingers across the bottle's glass surface, she spelt out 'J..A..C..K..D..A..N..I..E..L..S...BEST...MALT...WHISKEY.'

'We'll take it,' said a priest snatching the bottle and putting it deep inside his robes. 'It is a medicine worthy of our Almighty Saviour! Come brothers! We must go! Where's the Blue Dog?'

The priest who had so quickly taken the bottle, roused the little Blue Dog and clipped a lead to its collar. Patting the dog affectionately on the head he led it out and guided it away from the huddle of plastic tents. Chanting 'Malus spicatum et nostrum verdammt!' the other five priests followed eagerly behind – the Chaothic Path to God, it seemed, now had some direction to it.

*

'Your finger!'

'What's going on?' Susan asked genuinely surprised.

'New rules.' the woman Morality Guardian replied coldly.

'What rules?' Susan asked with an ever-so-slight hint of defiance in her voice.

'You want to question me?' the MG threatened and she suggested with icy authority, 'If you'd prefer we can always do this back at headquarters?'

After several days sitting alone and thinking in her flat, Susan had finally opened her rucksack and begun to pack. She knew she was at a cross-roads in herself and, rather than plodding straight on like a blinkered cart horse, she had decided to seriously change the direction of her life – finding grubby items of news to fill the empty spaces between the ears of bored people, was not an occupation she could ever come to accept. She may have to live a poor life, always scraping by, always fighting for clothes in jumble sales, but she would at least live it with a real taste of freedom in her mouth.

After she had made her decision to quit the city, Susan decided to visit a few friends one last time to say goodbye. She was on her way to see Bev – one of her closest friends – when she had turned a corner and almost collided with a woman Morality Guardian. The uniformed figure of authority was not pleased and ordered Susan to line up. She asked why, but the MG ignored her and shouted to the other women to move up and close the gaps. There were about six or so women in front of Susan and quietly she asked the woman in front of her in the queue, what was happening.

'It's the new test.' the woman whispered back from beneath her jiba.

'What test?' Susan asked. But the woman either didn't hear or was too frightened to say anything as she didn't answer Susan's question. The queue went down quickly and that is when the medical Morality Guardian had demanded Susan present her finger or do the test back at headquarters.

'No! No!' Susan replied alarmed, and with as much innocent sweetness as she could fake, she continued, ' No, I'm sorry, it's just that I haven't heard of any new rules. Owch!' Susan cried as the Guardian pricked her finger and smeared a tiny drop of blood across a pink strip of paper.

'Came into force at mid-night. You should have received a leaflet. Anyway, the test shows you've been menstruating for four days. You are unmarried?'

'Err yes.'

'And you are a virgin?'

'What do you need to know that for!?' Susan blurted out totally astonished.

'Don't question me!' barked the Guardian.

'Sorry! Yes...yes a virgin.'

'Wear this!' The Warden slapped a large white circle onto the sweater of Susan's upper arm, adding, 'And make sure it doesn't come off until your period is over! Next!'

Susan continued on her way to Bev's flat unable to believe she was now advertising to the world that she was a menstruating virgin! She looked around the street and, sure enough, of all the women she saw, each one now had a large coloured circle on their upper arm. Some had blue circles, some red, and a few wore the same large white circle she had – so they too were menstruating virgins! Unbelievable! But what did the other colours mean!?

*

'Daddy?' Rosie asked with a voice that hinted something was wrong.

'What is it Rosie?'

'It's those bright lights – they've come back.'

Dawn over the city dump was never a joyous affair, for the only light that rose in the stomachs of the people who lived there was hunger. And this morning was no exception. The night before – like far too many nights – the children had gone to bed hungry and malnourished. They had found some rubbish bags containing left-over rice but after it had all been shared out there had hardly been a mouthful for each child. And so, naturally, in the morning they had woken up hungry and, as usual, had gone off across the mountains of refuse in search of something to eat.

Rosie, however, lingered behind. She looked like she was suffering. Dark rings had suddenly appeared beneath her eyes. At first her father thought it was because of the lack of sleep and the constant hunger. But when Rosie said she could now see the shinning lights even when her eyes were open, he started to get worried. Ten minutes later she collapsed.

'Rosie!!'

Her father and mother rushed out and lifted Rosie from the ground and brought her limp form into the shelter.

'Rosie! Wake up!' they pleaded, but it was no use. They shook her gently, but Rosie's head just flopped from side to side.

'Is she still breathing?' her mother asked desperately.

'Yes, yes! O Rosie darling! Don't die!' her father cried and tears began to fall down his cheeks.

'Father!' Rosie's mother said with anger, 'We need a doctor, not tears!'

'I'm sorry – yes, you're right.' he answered wiping his eyes on his sleeve. 'I'll use that old rusty wheel-barrow. Quick get some cardboard to cover the holes in the bottom and we'll use some old cushions for a matrass.'

They lifted Rosie and gently lowered her onto a few broken cushions in the bottom of the wheel-barrow. Then they covered her with old clothes – jumpers, coats – anything to keep her warm for the journey. Rosie's mother stood up and straightened her back – her heavily pregnant belly was clearly causing a lot of pain. She then waddled quickly to one of the other shelters and returned with a bag of stale bread, a small bottle of water and a half-rotten orange. She placed them in the barrow near Rosie's feet and covered them with an old coat.

'Father – you find a good doctor for my Rosie, y'hear?'

He hugged his wife, his heart on fire with desperation and fear, and he promised to do everything possible to help their darling Rosie – even though he knew he had no idea where to go, who to ask or how to pay. A doctor was a luxury they had never needed – until now. Carefully he lifted the barrow up onto its wheel and set off down the path that led to the city – all the time trying his utmost to avoid the bumps and holes.

*

Susan quickly rang the bell three times – she was clearly in a hurry. Her friend Beverly opened the door.

'Susan! What's the big rush!?'

'I'm sick of this!' she pulled off her jiba and threw it to the floor. 'And this!' Susan pointed to the white circle stuck on the arm of her sweater. She tore it off and threw it across the hall. 'I'm sick of being treated like a piece of livestock!'

'Come in and sit down. We need to talk.' Beverly said quietly as she closed the front door. The two women went into the small kitchen, brewed some tea and sat down.

'Bev, how did it get like this?'

'Apathy I guess, nobody cared so nobody noticed.'

'Noticed what?'

'That we were trying to accommodate so many things, so many cultures, and no one spoke out.'

'But why not for heaven's sake!' Susan asked angrily.

'Because no one wanted to be called a racist, or a fascist. Have you seen this?' Beverly asked holding up an eye-catching leaflet.

'That must be the leaflet that cow mentioned.'

'Yep. Just listen to this.' Beverly held up the glossy leaflet and read aloud...

'The Grand Council Of Elders is pleased to announce a Great Leap Forward in the Emancipation of Women. The Menstrual Status Act – hereafter called Menstrual Curfew Ordinance 265 – decrees that all pre-menopausal women must remain at home, in-doors, for the first two days of their menstrual cycle. However, if they leave their home on the third day, they are required under the new Ordinance, to wear the appropriate 'Insignia of Honour'. The Insignia will take the shape of circles with a diameter of not less than six inches and will be worn on the upper right arm. The various categories of the said Insignia are hereby declared:

- *a woman who has been menstruating for 3 days or more, is required to wear a red circle.*
- *a woman who is a menstruating virgin is required to wear a white circle.*
- *a woman who is a non-menstruating virgin is required to wear a blue circle.*
- *a married woman who is pregnant is required to wear a gold circle.*

- *an unmarried woman who is pregnant is required to wear a black circle with a white cross.*

The Insignia of Honour will enhance the status of women in society providing them with greater equality, opportunity and security. The Menstrual Curfew Ordinance 265 has the blessing of Our Almighty Lord God, Saviour and Protector of Morality – by order of The Grand Council of Elders of The Temple of The Blue Dog, '.'

When Beverly finished she looked at Susan. Neither woman spoke. Beverly turned her head and stared through the window into space. Eventually, as though following a train of thought of her own, Beverly asked,

'What's the opposite of emancipation?'

'Slavery and a life of fear.' Susan slowly replied.

'And the opposite of equality?' Beverly continued.

'Bitterness and resentment.'

'And what's the opposite of opportunity?'

'A wasted life,' Susan replied grimly.

'So what do you call something that brings into law the very opposite of what it proclaims?' Beverly asked bitterly.

'An outright lie.' Susan immediately answered. Beverly nodded. There was a pause. Then with desperate determination Susan added -

'I can't stay here, in this city. I can't live like this. Next they'll be branding and stoning women in public. Every day it gets worse.'

'They *are* branding women.'

'What!?' Susan cried with disbelief.

'Maybe not in public. What this leaflet doesn't tell you Susan, is that there is another new Ordinance which – get this – allows them to surgically cauterise the clitoris of any woman they consider a risk to the sexual morality of society.' Beverly explained.

'Cauterise? What's that?' Susan asked almost breathless.

'They place a red-hot iron against the clitoris and burn it off.'

'NO!....NO!...It's....O my god! It's inhuman! It's barbaric! It's – '

'It's now the law.' Beverly finished.

'They BURN it off!?' Susan asked still unable to grasp the reality of what Beverly had said, and she continued passionately, 'But surly the doctors have refused? Surly there have been protests? riots? marches? boycotts?'

Beverly shook her head.

'The authorities say they're doing it for moral and cultural reasons and no one is objecting because no one wants to be labelled a racist.'

Susan shook her head not knowing what to say, she then remembered Bev's partner.

'How's Raneesha?' she asked quietly. Beverly looked away and Susan watched her eyes begin to glisten with tears. Susan reached across the kitchen table and took Beverly's hand.

'She's terrified,' Beverly answered through her tears.

'I'm sorry, I shouldn't have asked.'

'No, no...it's alright. She's all I can really think about. I think about her so much she becomes like a presence in the room. I never thought I would ever meet someone who loved me as totally as I loved them...but I did. The nights are so...lonely.'

'But you can't live apart like this – it's...it's wrong.'

'She's terrified her family will find out – if they did she'd either be sent back to Malakstan to marry some toothless hill farmer, or killed to uphold the family honour.'

'Can't you just be discreet?'

'We have been, but seeing each other once a month is breaking my heart, and Raneesha's a mess too. Her father and mother are now talking about arranging a marriage with some guy up in Bewcastle. She's totally freaked – and so am I.'

'Bev, listen!' Susan suddenly began. 'I really came here to say goodbye. I'm leaving this place tomorrow. Why don't you come with? You can send for Raneesha later! We'll make an escape plan. You can't honestly stay here Bev and live like this. We're being treated like animals! I know I can't stand it anymore! What you and Raneesha are going through doesn't bare thinking about! Come with!'

'I can't Susan – for one thing, I couldn't leave Raneesha now with her parents trying to marry her off to some stranger, and for another, I've just started a new teaching job. If I walked away now I'd never get another. Primary teaching is one of the last careers left for women. But, more to the point, where are *you* going? How will you live?'

'I'm lucky – I have an aunt – Auntie Jane – who lives in a small village outside the city. Her husband died some years ago and she's alone. She has five or six acres, so I'm hoping she'll welcome any help she can get. The village is very quiet. The women don't wear the jiba – only if some official, or Blue Dog priest is passing through – which hardly ever happens as the road into the place is a dead end.'

'But Susan you'll be so isolated. How will you live?'

'Better to live isolated and free, than having your clit burnt off. They must be mad! How will I live? I don't know, but live I will!'

*

Rosie's father had been pushing the wheel-barrow for over an hour. He was sweating and his arm and leg muscles were sore. He knew that somehow he had to find the strength to keep going. However, every time he glanced down at Rosie lying so pitifully unconscious, he felt a surge of energy so forceful he knew he would let nothing stop him from getting Rosie to a doctor. It was his love for this special child that fuelled his determination.

By now they had left the city dump far behind and were approaching an eight-lane motorway. As the traffic was so dense it was impossible to cross between the cars, so Rosie's father looked for the nearest bridge over the motorway and headed in that direction. Pushing the barrow uphill was always the hardest, so when he reached the middle of the bridge he stopped to get back his breath and have a small drink of water. He noticed that although the north bound carriageway was streaming with incessant traffic, the south bound was empty. Then he saw why. A line of half a dozen police cars, lights flashing, were blocking each of the four south bound lanes and behind them were four lines of cars stretching back mile after mile as far as the eye could see. But what Rosie's father saw in front of the police cars was a most extraordinary thing – there was a large, complete circle of blue-robed priests all lying face down on the motorway and, running around inside the circle, were three Blue Dogs play-fighting, chasing each other, rolling over and having a real merry time.

This was, people were later told on the news, a truly auspicious, truly sacred conjunction of three strands of Chaothicism – a meeting of three Blue Dogs in one place, people were assured, symbolised the Holy Trinity of the First, the Second and the Third Levels of Divine Will, thus demonstrating the real power of Chaos as the one-and-only True Force of God's Benevolent Nature.

As Rosie's father stood on the bridge watching the bizarre spectacle, another older man came and watched not far from where Rosie's father stood.

'Fucking stupid.' he commented to no one.

Rosie's father glanced at the man and answered while still looking down at the frolicking Blue Dogs, 'It does seem a bit silly.'

'Silly?' the older man questioned. He looked at Rosie's father and said, 'Makes less sense than pissin' int' t'wind! Country's gone mad!'

Then he noticed Rosie.

'What's with child?'

Rosie's father explained that he was urgently looking for a doctor for Rosie. They talked a bit and clearly the older man was touched by the sight of poor Rosie lying, apparently asleep, in a rusty old wheel-barrow and her desperate father. He rubbed his chin and then told Rosie's father to follow him up the road to the other side of the bridge where his pick-up was parked and he would give them a lift.

'I'm goin' int' t'town meself – I'll take yuz t'a place where there's a muckle load o'quacks! It's a place called Farley Street – right famous it is – ever 'eard of it?' he asked. Rosie's father, of course, hadn't ever heard of 'Farley Street', but the older man told him not to worry as he was sure to find someone there who could help Rosie.

Together they carefully lifted the wheel-barrow into the back of the man's pick-up. Rosie's father also sat in the back and was told to hold the barrow steady especially when going around corners. He climbed up next to Rosie and this pure act of kindness from a complete stranger made the flame of hope burn a little brighter in his heart.

About an hour later they were driving through some seriously busy streets in the heart of the city. Then the pick-up suddenly pulled over next to some faceless, glass pyramid and the older man got out and helped Rosie's father lift the barrow down onto the pavement. He told Rosie's father that Farley Street wasn't far away. It was, he said, a few blocks somewhere to the right but he couldn't drive there because of the expensive congestion charges. He wished Rosie and her father luck and drove off.

What a sight it was! A man with long, unwashed hair, bare-footed, wearing a dirty, grey T-shirt and ragged trousers, pushing his sick child in a rusty wheel-barrow through crowds of elegant people. Almost every well-dressed person was having a deep conversation into a phone pressed to their ear. They may have been untouched by poverty, but nonetheless, they did seem like they were addressing some important misery of their own.

Rosie's father's face strained as he pushed the barrow along the pavement deeper and deeper into this strange human desert. His dark eyes seemed to glow with an uncanny mixture of anger, hope, fear and confusion. Since he couldn't read the street signs he asked a few people where Farley Street was, but – thinking he was begging for money – they mostly ignored him and walked on pretending they hadn't noticed.

Finally, after walking around several streets and getting nowhere, Rosie's father approached a policeman who frowned suspiciously at Rosie lying unconscious in the barrow.

'I'm looking for Farley Street?'

'Well you needn't look any further – you're in it. This is Farley Street. What do you want here?'

'I'm looking for a doctor for my Rosie.'

'Pheeew!' was all the policeman said as he turned and walked away shaking his head.

Rosie's father looked up at the rows and rows of houses with their spotless white walls, railings and heavy, intimidating, black doors. Where to start? There were shiny brass plates beside every door but he could read none of them. Which would be the right one for Rosie? He didn't even know what was wrong with her. She had complained of 'seeing lights' – and they were almost the last words she had spoken.

He pushed Rosie up and down the street several times always looking up at the doors and windows hoping something would become clear. But tired and exasperated at getting this far and reaching a dead end, Rosie's father parked the wheel-barrow on the pavement in front of him, sat down on some steps, and buried his head in his hands trying to think of what to do next.

*

By the time Susan left Bev's flat to walk home it was already dark. To avoid any hassle from the MG's she had stuck the white circle back on her arm. However, it soon became apparent she had made a big mistake because, not five minutes after leaving Bev's place, she was being followed by a small group of about three men who immediately started shouting obscenities.

'Hey! Virgin girl!'

'Horny bitch! Come here!'

Susan walked faster and crossed the road to where the lights from the shops were brighter. But the men did the same and she noticed there were now four or five of them and one was using his phone. Somehow she felt they were not going to leave her alone. She began to get seriously frightened. She turned a corner. There in front of her were two men one of whom was also on his phone. This was dangerous. Susan felt a wave of fear hit her in the stomach. She stopped. Immediately a large hand came from nowhere and wrapped itself over her mouth. She tried to scream but it was impossible. She was dragged into an unlit passageway between two shops. The darkness suddenly seemed to fill with men grabbing at her body and clothes. She tried to lash out but her hands were being firmly held from behind. A hand groped at her breast and ripped open the side of her tunic. Susan began shaking her head violently from side to side thinking she might loosen the grip of the hand over her mouth, but it was no use.

'Get the bitch down! Open her legs!'

Susan felt her legs being forced apart and just as she was about to collapse with the unspeakable terror of being gang-raped, a beam of light pierced the darkness of the alleyway and a burst of machinegun fire raked across the walls. Susan fell to the ground and heard her attackers scatter. There was another burst of machinegun fire and then silence. She heard slow footsteps and the beam of light became stronger. Then a man's voice said,

'Get up.'

Susan got slowly to her feet shaking with fear. She clutched her torn clothes to her body. She looked up into the torch beam and winced at the glaring light. The beam was lowered and she recognised the uniform of a regular policeman.

'Come on – let's get you to the station.'

'I'm...I'm alright...I ...I just need to get home.' Susan whispered with a frightened, trembling voice.

'I'm sorry, this is a serious incident, you'll have to come to the station and give a statement. Don't worry, it's not far.'

Susan was in no state to argue and right now a police station felt a safer place to be than alone in her flat. A small crowd had gathered attracted by the sound of the automatic gun fire and they stood and stared as the policeman and Susan walked away side by side. Some women and children and a few men began pointing at her because she was the only woman out on the street with her face exposed – she had lost her jiba during the struggle. But the presence of the policeman kept them at bay.

When they arrived at the station the policeman let Susan use the women officer's bathroom and take a shower. A policewoman brought her a towel, some replacement clothes and a new jiba. When she was ready another policewoman led her to an interview room and brought her a cup of tea. A few minutes later the same policewoman returned together with a small, uniformed, squat man wearing very circular, black-rimmed glasses. He introduced himself as DC Whitehead.

'Well now young lady, it seems you were very lucky tonight,' he stated. Susan said nothing. She was still in a state of shock. Her mind was numb with so many awful feelings she couldn't think straight. The officer sensed this and so concentrated on the practicalities. He went through the formality of filling out the statement form, taking Susan's name and address, her age etcetera, and even helped her to reconstruct step by step what had happened.

When they had finished Susan asked if she could be taken home. However, the officer spread his hands on the table, and chose his words carefully,

'As matters stand, we have only your account of the incident and a written statement from the officer who found you. So, as required by law, I have sent out several officers to the area where the alleged assault took place and they are looking for witnesses – even trying to track down those who you say attacked you. So under the circumstances, while my men are gathering evidence, it is probably safer for you to remain here with us overnight.'

'But!...' Susan began. The officer held up his hand and stopped her.

'Don't worry! – we'll look after you. We have a special overnight room for cases like this. It's very cosy. There's a TV and we can even get hold of a counsellor should you need to talk to someone. We won't lock you up in the cells! After all you've done nothing wrong,' he laughed.

Susan felt too distraught, too powerless to object, and anyway they did seem to be treating her with a lot of consideration. At this moment, all she really wanted, was to lie down and rest, to sleep and forget, to fall into a darkness where she could try and banish the dreadful images in her mind. So she consented – even though she wasn't entirely sure if she was free to go or not.

*

Across the street, not far from where Rosie's father sat, a two-man film crew were interviewing someone of obvious importance judging from the clothes they wore and the way they were gesticulating in front of the camera. But for some reason the interview finished abruptly and the important person turned and walked off down Farley Street as though annoyed. The reporter and cameraman exchanged a few words and burst out laughing. The reporter then looked at his watch and was just about to turn away when he caught sight of Rosie's father sitting on the steps to one of the surgeries. However, what really excited his attention was the wheel-barrow on the pavement with one of Rosie's little hands flopping over the side. The reporter tapped the cameraman on the arm, crossed the street and introduced himself to Rosie's father.

'Hello. My name's Damian McAllister from BCB News. Would you like to be live on breakfast TV? We could do a quick interview. You can tell your story – where you're from, why you're here – that sort of thing. It'll only take a few minutes?....'

On the first floor of the surgery where Rosie's father was sitting, Doctor Abdulla-Smith was secretly peeping through the blinds down at what was happening outside. He pressed the TV remote in his hands and flicked through various news channels. After a few misses he found it. On the TV was the face of the reporter who, at that very moment, was standing outside Dr. Abdulla-Smith's own surgery.

'Today, as I stand in one of the most prestigious and famous medical streets in the world, it is well to remember that there are others in this city not so fortunate. I have beside me Mr. Harrison who has come many miles on foot to find help for his sick child Rosie...'

The camera turned to show Rosie lying pale and limp in the wheel-barrow. Then Rosie's father's face appeared on the screen...

'My Rosie just fell down. I don't know what to do. She's real sick...'

Dr. Abdulla-Smith glanced at the scene down in the street and rubbed his chin. Suddenly he snapped his fingers, ran from the window and bolted down the stairs to the front door. Swinging the door wide open he flew, like some saviour of all humankind, down the steps to where the filming was happening.

'Welcome! Welcome!' he loudly exclaimed and opening his arms continued, 'Charity is the jewel of civilisation! Mr. Harrison I'm so pleased to meet you! And this is Rosie? – Let's get her inside.' The Doctor turned and clapped his hands at two assistants who were standing confused in the open doorway.

'Quickly! Take Rosie upstairs to the examination room!'

The two assistants ran down the steps and gently lifted Rosie's lifeless form out of the wheel-barrow. Gingerly they carried her up the steps and disappeared inside.

'May I ask your name Doctor?' the reporter Damian asked.

'Yes! Of course!' Dr. Abdulla-Smith turned and beamed into the camera, 'I'm Dr. Abdulla-Smith, FRCP, FRCS, MSc, PhD, Professor of General Paediatrics at University College and Associate Professor of Blue Dog Theology at Oxford!'

'Wow that's impressive! But tell me Professor, why are you helping this poor man Mr. Harrison who is, after all, an Untouchable from the Roja caste?'

'Why am I helping him?' the Doctor repeated raising his eyebrows as though astonished at the question. Then he smiled straight at the camera and continued magnanimously, 'Because it is my duty to assist the poor. It's all very well for me to have the most outstanding medical practice in Farley Street, caring for the health and well-being of Royalty, of the Rich and Famous, but as a devoted student of the new theology, I know God wants me to use my considerable talents to cure all who are sick – especially sick children like Rosie. Now if you'll excuse me, I must get Mr. Harrison up to my consultation room – we have important work to do.' Here Doctor Abdulla-Smith put his arm around Rosie's father who had, all this time, been standing confused and silent but happy that at last something was being done to help Rosie. The Doctor again smiled effusively at the camera, turned and led Mr. Harrison up the steps and through the large doorway into the surgery. But just before closing the door the good Doctor called out to Damian and the cameraman who were still filming –

'You can find all my details at 'doctorabdullasmith.com'!'

The large, weighty, black door closed. Then the letter box suddenly opened and the doctor shouted through the gap –

'All one word!'

*

The next morning Susan was woken by someone knocking gently on the door to her room.

'Hello?' she called out with a sleepy voice.

'Are you awake? Can I come in?' a woman's voice asked.

'Yes...yes it's OK.' Susan replied remembering she was in a police station. A policewoman entered with a small tray.

'Here, I've brought you a little breakfast.'

'Oh? Thanks.'

'How are you?' the other woman asked.

'OK I guess.'

'Listen, I think you ought to know – there've been some developments in your case last night and DC Whitehead wants to interview you, just to clarify a few points, as soon as you've finished breakfast – let's say in about twenty minutes? – Oh and don't forget your jiba.'

'Sure.'

After she had dressed, washed and had breakfast, all that Susan really wanted was to get back to her flat, finish her packing and say goodbye to this city and all the misogynist cruelty it tolerated. Another interview, she argued, wouldn't take long and then she could get home.

Twenty minutes later the policewoman returned and led Susan back to the interview room. This time, however, she was flanked by two uniformed policewomen she hadn't seen before. They stood either side of her behind her chair. When Susan entered DC Whitehead was already seated. On the table before him were several papers. Without looking up he asked Susan to please sit down, but there was something in the tone of his voice which made Susan feel uneasy.

'As you know,' he began, 'last night we made extensive enquiries in the neighbourhood where the incident took place. I'm sorry to have to ask you this but did you at any time provoke or consent to the rape?'

'What? I don't understand? I told you – I was followed, I was attacked. I was almost raped.' Susan stated trying to understand the question.

'Yes, that's your version of events.' DC Whitehead replied.

'And how does a woman 'consent' to be raped? – it makes no sense!' Susan blurted out not listening.

'You see Zariah Law is quite clear about this,' DC Whitehead continued, 'If a woman provokes or consents to the rape it carries an automatic prison sentence of thirty days with no right of habeas corpus. However, if the man – or, in your case, men – admits the crime of rape, he is honour bound to pay you £50. But if, on the other hand, the man denies the rape, the woman who has brought the charge, must receive fifty lashes for questioning the man's honour and wasting police time. Now in your case Susan we have established that there were no witnesses to the alleged attempted rape, but we did find three men who said they were with you in the alleyway. They claim that you were looking for sex. That you stopped and let them take you into the alleyway to have intercourse.'

'WHAT!?' Susan jumped out of her chair. The two policewomen behind restrained her and made her sit down.

'That's rubbish! It's a pack of lies!' Susan shouted unable to believe what she was hearing.

'And furthermore,' DC Whitehead continued like a steam-roller, 'one of the men said you paid him £20 to have sex and – '

'LIES! LIES! LIES!' Susan screamed from behind her jiba.

'It's fortunate for you, however, that this morning another man came to the station and volunteered a different version of events which, to some extent, supports your own. This leaves me in a difficult position. Three men deny the attack, yet one man admits his part in assault. The only fair conclusion I've reached, under Zariah Law, is that you should be paid £20 by the man who supports your version, but you should also spend three days in custody and receive 25 lashes on the morning of your release.' DC Whitehead stood up to leave. Susan leapt from her chair like a tigress only to be gripped and forced to sit by the two policewomen behind her.

'WHAT!? You can't do this!' Susan roared, 'I was attacked! I did nothing wrong!! I'm innocent!!' But DC Whitehead had already left the room without listening.

*

'This is an MRI scan of Rosie's head. I looked here first because you said Rosie had been seeing bright lights even when fully awake.'

Mr. Harrison – Rosie's father – was sitting in a darkened room looking at a screen that spanned an entire wall. First Rosie's enormous sleeping face had appeared, then her skin vanished and her white skull appeared. The pale white bone then faded away and revealed Rosie's brain magnified at least ten times its normal size. The detail that could be seen was miraculous. Doctor Abdulla-Smith stood in front of the image and continued –

'You can see here and here that part of Rosie's brain responsible for sight and as you can see here, this is an abnormal growth. Put bluntly, it shouldn't be there. It's starting to press against the part that controls Rosie's sight, and that is, without doubt, the cause of the bright lights. This abnormal growth, Mr. Harrison, is called a tumour. Sometimes they are easy to remove but sometimes the operation can prove fatal. It all depends on how the tumour has grown. If it's grown in a complicated way then the surgeon will only be able to partially remove it. In which case it will more than likely regrow and the patient will eventually die. If, on the other hand, the tumour has grown in a simple fashion, attached to only one tiny part of the brain tissue, then it is often easy for the surgeon to remove it and the patient will make a full recovery. However, the problem we face is that often we can only tell what type of tumour it is, once we have opened up the patient's brain and the surgeon can see it with his own eyes and so assess what to do. Given my experience of judging tumours from MRI scans, I seriously think Rosie is in grave danger and needs an operation to remove the tumour as soon as possible – I would say tomorrow or the day after at the very latest. Any longer and we might lose her. I hope I'm not going too fast for you Mr. Harrison, but Rosie's case is an emergency.'

'No...no I don't want to lose Rosie. You would do this operation?'

'Me?! No, not at all. I want the best for Rosie. An old friend of mine, Professor Henry Marshal, is a world famous neurosurgeon. He is an expert in this sort of surgery – especially on children. I'm not sure he is in the country at the moment, but let's see if I can get hold of him – it's worth a try!'

Dr. Abdulla-Smith picked up the phone on his desk and dialled. After less than ten seconds he was put through.

'Henry! You're still here! No! No, I thought you might be away on one of your Balkan trips? Ah in June! Wonderful! Listen I'll come straight to the point. I have a six year old Roja girl with what appears to be an advanced benign astrocytoma pressing against the right visual cortex. The patient became unconscious early this morning and I was wondering if you could fit her in for surgery either sometime tomorrow or the day after – her situation is critical...Yes?...Of course,

I can email you the scans within the next half an hour...Splendid! Henry you're a marvel!...Once I've sorted out some details with the father I'll get her over to you by ambulance. She should be with you within the hour. Thanks again! Yes, we'll speak soon, bye.'

The Doctor beamed at Rosie's father.

'There, that's sorted! Connections in this profession are so important. Let's just get the transport arranged.'

Doctor Abdulla-Smith clicked an intercom switch on the wall near to where he was standing.

'Sir?' a man's voice asked.

'Yes, Baker. Can you prepare Rosie for emergency transit to St. Mary's? We'll use the chopper it's faster.'

'Right away sir.'

'Thank you.' The Doctor then addressed Rosie's father.

'There, that's done – she'll be on her way soon.'

He then coughed and sat down at his desk opposite Rosie's father.

'Now, Mr. Harrison, this brings us to the rather delicate matter of payment. Since you are a Roja, we'll have to assume you do not possess the financial means to cover the costs of Rosie's treatment.'

'How much would that cost be?' asked Rosie's father anxiously.

'That is an impossible question to answer Mr. Harrison. You see, it's not just the cost of the operation itself – which can be considerable – it is the post-operative costs to consider – the costs of Intensive Care, the costs of ongoing medication, more MRI scans, occupational therapy. Then Rosie will need weeks, maybe months, in a convalescence home. This all costs money I'm afraid. If I had to put a ball-park figure on it I'd say we were looking at about five hundred thousand pounds – maybe more. After the operation she will need a lot of care and attention from advanced intensive care technicians. So there can be no question of Rosie returning to her old life as a Roja – the risks of infection would be enormous.'

Here Doctor Abdulla-Smith paused as though trying to find the right words. He reached out and fiddled with a pen on his desk, then slowly he began,

'There is, however, another possibility, one which you might find difficult to accept, but the benefits to Rosie would be huge. What I'm asking you to do Mr. Harrison, is to put Rosie's future interests, her future well-being, first. I know a parent's love and bond to their child can be immense – I fully understand that, but even so that child will grow up and one day leave home. So in another 10 or so years Rosie will leave – she'll meet someone or get a job in another city. What I am proposing – with your full agreement, of course – is that you let Rosie come and...and live with me so that I can look after her. This means I would meet all the costs of her treatment – the operation and all post-op costs and requirements – you would pay nothing. She is a pretty child who – if she survives – will, one day I'm sure, grow up to be an asset to any man. Am I making much sense Mr. Harrison?'

'You want her as your own child?' Rosie's father asked in a voice that was almost a whisper.

'No...no, I don't want to adopt her as my daughter, that's not what I meant,' replied the Doctor looking directly at Rosie's father for the first time.

'Then I don't understand what you mean?'

'I would like...I would like Rosie to be my wife – but of course, only when she reaches the age of eight years as required under Zariah Law.'

'I...I can't do that!' Rosie's father said astonished.

'I thought you might say that.' The Doctor said in a rather flat voice. Then he leant forward and clicked the intercom on his desk.

'Sir?'

'Baker, could you just hold Rosie's move to St. Mary's – there's been a little hic-up with the paper work.'

'Of course, sir.'

'I'm not sure Mr. Harrison that you really have Rosie's best interests at heart. Think about the benefits for Rosie. I have two other wives, both younger than me of course but still fully mature – one is 17 and the other is 28 – they would both love and take care of Rosie like she was their own child. You would, of course, be free to see Rosie at any time. You could even think of this arrangement as a second home for Rosie. With me she would never know hunger again, she would have her own centrally-heated room with an en-suit bathroom, have her own wardrobe of clothes, go to the hairdresser, she would never have to cook or clean, she would travel abroad, see the world. Also you mentioned she was clever, that she'd taught herself to read? Well, I would ensure that she received one of the finest educations in the world and go to one of the top universities. All this, and more, I can guarantee. What, Mr Harrison, can you offer? A life of constant hunger verging on starvation? A life eating rotten or half-rotten food? A life of disease and infection? No education? No opportunities? Living like a rodent? Slowly dying from cold, heat and sickness? Surely you can see that's not a life for a child with Rosie's talents Mr. Harrison? Please seriously consider this proposal – for Rosie's sake.'

'I don't know...I didn't expect...My wife? I'll have to see what Helena thinks about this.' Rosie's father replied his emotions and thoughts swirling around inside him like some incomprehensible whirlpool.

'Of course you must.' The Doctor stood up. 'Listen, I've got an important guest arriving in ten minutes and – ' Rosie's father realised it was time to go so he too got up. Talking slowly the Doctor walked with Rosie's father to the door of the consultation room.

'Why don't we do it this way Mr. Harrison – while you go back and talk it over with your wife, I'll send Rosie over to St. Mary's for the operation – that way she will be out of any immediate danger. That's the important thing. Then, when you're ready, come back and see me and I'm sure we'll be able to sort something out.'

'So, you'll look after my Rosie till I get back?'

'Of course, you have my word.' the Doctor replied as he opened the door and led Rosie's father out into the hallway. Standing outside was one of the Doctor's assistants.

'Ah Baker! Good! You can take Rosie to St. Mary's right away.'

'Yes sir.'

'And tell Jones to come and speak to Mr. Harrison – he'll know what to do.'

'Right away sir.' Baker disappeared and the Doctor turned to Rosie's father and said,

'I'm handing you over to my assistant Jones – he's a good man – he'll explain what you now need to do – I'm sure it won't take more than an hour, if that – then he'll drive you home. It's been a pleasure talking to you Mr. Harrison and I look forward to meeting you again very soon.'

Rosie's father held out his hand, but the good Doctor took a step backwards and shook his head saying,

'I'm awfully sorry Mr. Harrison, but I can't...not yet...Jones will explain,' and he turned and went back into his consultation room and closed the door.

*

The cell Susan found herself in was really a large room containing about a dozen bunk-beds. There were three bare, windowless walls but the fourth wall was just iron bars from floor to ceiling. As he opened a gate in the bars, the prison warden told Susan to choose a bunk in the corner where it would be less draughty.

As soon as the warden had left Susan was immediately surrounded by about ten women (none of whom were wearing a jiba) who wanted to know who she was? what she had done? where she was from? what was her punishment? and a dozen more questions that Susan tried her best to answer. Then one of the women put her arms around Susan and gave her probably one of the most welcoming hugs Susan had ever had, and, stupid though it must sound, within minutes Susan felt incredibly at ease and 'at home' in prison. However, because being in a prison was legally classed as 'forced domicile', it meant that, just as in their real homes women were not required to wear the jiba, so too here in prison. Hence, the first thing one of the women did was remove Susan's and throw it high in the air to the cheers and delight of all.

Many of the women, it appeared, had been picked up for infringing the newly introduced Menstrual Curfew Ordinance 265 – they'd worn the wrong Insignia or none at all. Some women had been denounced as prostitutes – by men they had never even met or heard of – or for behaving provocatively in public. One woman, for example, said she'd opened her arms wide and given a long lost friend a hug on the street – the MG on duty called this a gesture designed to provoke OED (Overt Erotic Desire), and so she was arrested. One woman told how a sudden gust of wind had blown off her jiba and she was immediately arrested for exposing her face. Another said she was arrested for wearing a pair of trousers underneath her durka – she'd told the MGs she'd worn them because it was cold, but they wouldn't listen. One woman showed Susan her bandaged finger and said she'd been stopped when one of the MGs had noticed her painted finger nails. They'd called her a provocative harlot and pulled out one nail with a pair of pliers as a warning, saying that if she was caught again she would lose all her fingernails.

For the first time in her life, here amongst these ordinary women, Susan felt a feeling of belonging and friendship with people who, like herself, were suffering under layer upon layer of repressive laws. Outside her prison walls, it was like one half of the human race, obsessed by dominance to the point of cruelty, had turned against the other half. How it had got like this she didn't know. Maybe, she thought, Bev was right, no one had cared enough and now it was too late.

On her second day of incarceration Susan was lying on her bunk thinking of her Auntie Jane working alone on her six acres, when she was approached by Tammy and Paula. Both were in their mid-twenties, one had brunette hair, the other blond. Susan had chatted with them on her first day behind bars and had struck up an instant friendship. The two women came and sat at the bottom of Susan's bunk and each glanced at the other as though they didn't know who should talk first. To dispel the hesitation Susan asked,

'What's up Tammy? Paula? What you after?'

'We were wondering if...if you would help us?' Tammy began.

'You see, you get out the same time as we do – the day after tomorrow.' Paula added.

'After we've had our lashes.' Tammy said grimacing.

'Humm I can't wait.' Susan answered sardonically and she asked, 'Help? Sure, with what?'

Then, lowering her voice and glancing around the cell, Tammy explained,

'Me and Paula, we've decided to stage a protest. We've arranged a rather special...' Tammy searched for the right words, so Paula helped and said,

'Dance routine.'

'A dance routine? But I can't dance.' Susan replied.

'You won't have to. We just want you to film us. We'll give you the camera. Show you what to do.'

'OK – that doesn't sound too difficult. But where are you going to do this special dance routine?'

'We haven't decided yet.'

'It's probably going to be in some high-profile public place.' Paula explained.

'OK, but when are you wanting to do this, because I was planning to leave the city as soon as I get out of here?'

'We're all to be released this Friday morning. How about meeting up on Saturday?' Tammy suggested.

'Sure. What time? Where?' Susan asked,

'Let's say 11am, outside Bicester Square tube?'

'But how will we recognise each other if we're all wearing jibas?' Susan asked.

'We'll be carrying rucksacks. You could wear a bright scarf?' Paula suggested.

'OK, I've got a bright red scarf – I'll wear that.' Susan agreed.

And so it was arranged. On her third and last day in prison Susan found herself becoming more and more intrigued at the thought of filming a protest. However, she had no idea of how much this simple act would change her plans of voluntary exile in the countryside, to exile as an everlasting fugitive.

On the morning of her release Susan was photographed and taken to another room. Her back was bared and she was held face down across a table. It was exactly what it was supposed to be – deeply humiliating. However, maybe because it was her first offence Susan was lucky because the 25 lashes she received, were not given brutally, they did not wound her flesh, they were just hard enough to sting. It was almost as though the man doing it had no real enthusiasm for whipping women's backs, but that, of course, could always change.

Susan was driven home back to her flat in a police car. When the car stopped outside, the woman police driver handed Susan a bag of coloured Insignia saying that if she must go out alone to always wear the purple patch with the yellow dot in the middle.

'What's that one mean?' Susan asked.

'Wear that one and you'll always be safe, no man will come near you. It means you have VD – venereal disease. Bye!'

*

'My employer Dr. Abdulla-Smith is a very pious, very devout man. He prays several times a day and eats only beetroot on Sundays.'

Jones and Rosie's father were being driven through the city streets by one of Dr. Abdulla-Smith's chauffeurs, and Jones was explaining why the Doctor had declined to shake his hand. It was, of course, because he, Mr. Harrison, was a Roja, an Untouchable. Jones explained that, before the operation to save Rosie's life could go ahead, all parties had to be rendered spiritually immaculate. This was necessary in order to purge the many demonic contaminants of the Roja caste. Once this was complete, then, and only then, was physical contact across the caste barrier possible. So for Rosie's treatment to proceed it was necessary for him, Mr. Harrison, to undergo a purification ritual at the Temple of the Blue Dog. The purification was needed not just for him, of course, but also for Rosie – he would be acting as Rosie's proxy so to speak, because, after all, she too was an Untouchable.

'So that's where we're going – to get you and Rosie purified. Don't be alarmed, I'll explain everything when we get there.'

'But where's my Rosie now?' Rosie's father asked with a worried voice.

'She's on her way to St. Mary's for her operation, but they won't admit her until your purification ritual is finished – it shouldn't take more than an hour,' Jones patted his smart phone that was peeping from the top of his jacket pocket and added, 'I'll let them know.'

After a ten minute drive they arrived at the Temple of the Blue Dog. Its enormity was just staggering. However, the one dominant feature that – almost like a magnet – drew people inside, was the immense central dome. Once they stood beneath it, the dome seemed to cast a spell over people's minds. They stopped talking, stopped thinking and just gazed upwards, mesmerised by the breath-taking space and shafts of multi-coloured sunlight entering from every direction. Then, if this was not enough, suspended from the very apex of the dome was a gigantic glass statue of the Blue Dog that glowed with an inner sapphire light.

Immediately below the statue, dressed in blue and lying spread-eagled on the floor of the temple, were groups of supplicants, who, instead of lying face down, lay face up, eyes wide, staring at the Blue Dog above them. The statue itself must have been at least ten meters high, and, because it was hanging by a transparent cable, it must have given the supplicants on the floor below the impression that the Blue Dog was really floating over their heads. The one, final spectacular effect, was that the huge statue was slowly rotating.

Jones walked ahead of Rosie's father and approached one of the Blue Priests who was obviously expecting him. They shook hands and exchanged a few words. The priest nodded and Jones turned and beckoned to Rosie's father to come over to meet the priest. Rosie's father took it for granted there would be no hand-shakes so he didn't offer his hand. The priest just smiled and, together with Jones, took Rosie's father to a small side-room away from the main temple space.

The priest told Rosie's father that he would be taken to a bathroom where he should perform his toilet and then take a shower – in that order. There was plenty of soap and shampoo provided and he should use as much as he wished. His ragged clothes he was to throw away in a red bin in the corner of the bathroom and, for the ceremony, to put on a small knee-length blue kilt that he would find on a chair. When he was ready he should ring a small bell that was next to the chair and another priest would come and escort him to the Grand Muftin for the purification ceremony.

The priest instructing Rosie's father took out a smart phone, tapped the screen and told him to wait there. The priest and Jones walked away chatting and laughing. A minute later another Blue-robed priest appeared and told Rosie's father to follow him. He was taken to a bathroom and left alone. He then did everything the priest had instructed him to do – although he did stand in the shower for longer than maybe he was allowed because he had never before had the experience of clean, warm water flowing down over his body – it was so delicious, so strange and so renewing.

When he was ready he rang the bell. As he stood waiting he saw himself in the mirror. He looked very peculiar indeed, more, he thought, like a middle-aged, skinny gorilla in a frilly thing. It was also exceedingly 'draughty' as the last instruction he'd received from the priest was to wear nothing – no underpants – beneath the kilt. What this bizarre get-up had to do with the path to purification he had no idea.

There was a knock at the bathroom door and the same priest entered and asked Rosie's father to follow him. Outside Rosie's father noticed that the supplicants beneath the central Blue Dog statue had all gone and in their place was a large circular screen with a small curtained entrance at the side. Halfway to the screen the priest stopped and, in whispered undertones, told Rosie's father that the entire purification ceremony with the Grand Muftin would take place behind the screen and he was to do all that the Grand Muftin instructed. The priest then nodded to someone and, when Rosie's father turned to look, he saw Jones standing in the shadows watching.

The priest then gestured to Rosie's father to continue on alone, whispering that, as he entered into the presence of the Grand Muftin, he was to bow respectfully and then do exactly as he was told.

Giving a low, respectful bow – just as he'd been instructed – Rosie's father pushed slowly through the curtained entrance. What he saw inside when he stood upright was an old man dressed in a blue, jewel-studded jacket and a golden hat that seemed to have two wings pointing vertically upwards above the Grand Muftin's ears. But to his astonishment the Grand Muftin also wore a short, blue kilt – presumably, Rosie's father thought uneasily, also with nothing on underneath.

'Welcome, my son,' the Grand Muftin sang. Rosie's father smiled not knowing if he should, or shouldn't, look directly at the odd figure before him.

'Don't be frightened. First I must teach you the chant of the Brotherhood which you must repeat several times when I tell you. Now repeat after me: 'Malus spicatum...' '

'Malus spicatum...' Rosie's father repeated.

'...et nostrum verdammt!'

'...et nostrum verdammt!'

'Very good. Now all together: 'Malus spicatum et nostrum verdammt!'

'Malus spicatum et nostrum verdammt!' repeated Rosie's father.

'Good. Now we must both go down on all fours. Come on, like this.' The Grand Muftin then got down on his knees and leant forward to support his head and torso with his hands on the floor – just like children do when they are pretending to be a four-legged animal. Completely bewildered, Rosie's father stood there unsure if this wasn't all some sort of joke, but no, with a firm voice the Grand Muftin ordered,

'Come, get down!'

Slowly Rosie's father descended onto all fours and found himself staring straight into the Grand Muftin's face.

'Now lick my nose.'

'What sir?' Rosie's father asked as though he hadn't heard properly. But, by way of an answer, the Grand Muftin suddenly lurched forwards and licked Rosie's father right across the nose and said smiling,

'There! Now it's your turn.'

'But...I've...er...I've never...' Rosie's father stammered as he sensed how wet and cold his nose was.

'I know it may seem strange – but these are the required rituals.'

Something buzzed inside the Grand Muftin's jewel-studded coat and he took out his phone.

'Yes, yes, so far so good. About ten minutes.' He answered into the phone. Then putting it away he said to Rosie's father, 'That was

Jones, just checking. Now, repeat 'Malus spicatum et nostrum verdammt! and lick my nose.'

Rosie's father thought about Jones, about Rosie, about what he was doing, but the message was clear – if he wanted to help Rosie he had to do as he was told. So, repeating 'Malus spicatum...' etcetera, he leant forwards and quickly licked the Grand Muftin's nose.

'Very good – that wasn't so bad was it? Now I'm going to turn around, expose my posterior and you must sniff my buttocks.' So saying the Grand Muftin shuffled around on all fours, flipped up his kilt and proffered up his naked backside.

'Sir! I ...I can't do this!' Rosie's father exclaimed.

'This is the last part of the ceremony! We're almost finished – you must complete the ritual!' ordered the Grand Muftin in a loud whisper over his shoulder.

'But sir I...I - '

'Do you want your daughter's operation cancelled?' the Grand Muftin threatened.

'No! No! Of course not!' Rosie's father said in a panic.

'Then sniff!' commanded the Grand Muftin.

Holding his breath and closing his eyes Rosie's father leant forwards to the pasty, sagging buttocks and sniffed loudly.

'More!' hissed the Grand Muftin, 'I must feel your nose in the cleavage between my buttocks – it's the only way!'

Thinking only of Rosie's welfare her father did as he was told – still with his eyes closed and holding his breath.

'Ahhh! That's better! Such bliss!' the Grand Muftin sighed.

The Grand Muftin turned around and stood up saying,

'Rise my son. You did well. The anal embodiment of Chaothicism is not an easy accomplishment, but you have surpassed all expectations. You have performed the secret rituals of purification with a spirit of true piety, and so, you and your daughter, have therefore been allowed to ascend a step closer to heaven. No longer will you be seen as Untouchables. You are now free to touch any caste above or below you. And, because you have surrendered your entire being to the Chaothic Way, both you and your daughter have been accepted into the faith of the Blue Dog. Welcome. However, you must not reveal the rituals you have seen today to any living soul – for if you do, you will fall from God's grace and expose your daughter to the evils of the cunning Devs – she could burst into flames at any second. Go in peace my son. Here, take this,' The Grand Muftin placed a small pendent of the Blue Dog around Rosie's father's neck. He then opened his arms, embraced Rosie's father and kissed him on the lips! The Grand Muftin led him to the curtained entrance in the screen, ushered him outside and signalled to Jones that he was ready. The shadowy Jones took out his phone, pressed the screen several times, said one word to whoever answered, and then dropped the phone back inside his top jacket pocket.

The Grand Muftin said goodbye and returned behind the screen. Another priest then arrived and, after congratulating him, took Rosie's father to a different side-room, gave him a clean shirt, a pair of trousers and some socks and shoes. When he'd changed into his new clothes, Jones took him outside to the car and told the chauffeur to take Mr. Harrison home.

'Welcome,' Jones said smiling and he offered Rosie's father his hand. Hesitantly Mr. Harrison shook Jones's hand and, for a fleeting moment, felt a tiny glimmer of genuine equality – something he had never before experienced in his life.

As Rosie's father got into the car, Jones told him not to worry, that Rosie had arrived safely at St. Mary's and, after some preliminary tests, she would soon be prepared for her operation. He said that Mr. Harrison should come back to the Farley Street surgery tomorrow to find out how Rosie's operation went. He closed the car door, tapped the shiny roof, and the chauffeur accelerated off into the city streets.

Rosie's father sat back and stared out of the window at the passing images of the city. He tried to make some sense of all that had happened to him that day. But his mind kept coming back over and over again to the same thing – if she survived the operation, Dr. Abdulla-Smith wanted Rosie as a child-bride. What would his wife Helena think of this? Everything the Doctor had said, of course, was true – Rosie's life would be transformed from abject poverty and deprivation, to one in which all her dreams and talents could be fulfilled...but was that enough of a reason to give up Rosie – especially a child whom he adored to the point of pain?

*

Saturday morning arrived and Susan was standing waiting on the pavement outside Bisceter tube station wearing her bright red scarf as agreed. It was a couple of minutes before eleven, and although there were crowds of people moving along the pavement and in and out of the tube station, Susan had already caught the eye of two Morality Guardians – simply because a woman standing alone, loitering, was highly suspicious. Through the eye-slit of her jiba Susan noticed they had started to film her as she pretended to look in the window of a kiosk. Then she saw two women coming up the stairs from the tube station carrying large, bulky rucksacks. She waved, relieved that her friends had arrived, and together they walked off and melted into the ever-moving crowds.

'Where are we heading?' Susan asked when they were well away from the MGs.

'We thought of Strafalgar Square, it's just down the road from here.' Tammy answered.

Although they were trying hard not to sound serious, Paula and Tammy didn't really talk much, they just plodded on and Susan was beginning to have misgivings about what exactly they were going to do. Carrying these heavy, frame rucksacks over their ankle-length robes and jibas, certainly didn't help to promote gaiety.

After five or ten minutes of solid trudging they arrived at Strafalgar Square. With obvious relief they took their rucksacks off and leant them against a low wall at the top of some steps that led down into the square. Tammy brought out a small video camera with, she explained, a very powerful zoom and she showed Susan the various settings. When Susan was ready Paula looked at her with intense, serious eyes and said,

'You promise that no matter what happens, no matter what you see, you will keep filming? You don't stop for anything – you understand?'

'Yes, of course, but why the large rucksacks? What have you got in them?' Susan asked.

'Speakers, a really powerful amp, a CD player and batteries – they weigh a ton,' Tammy replied.

'They're basically stage props,' Paula added.

'So you're dancing?' Susan queried.

'Yes. Do you know Britten's War Requiem?' Paula asked.

'I think I heard it once at school, ages ago – didn't he use poems from that war poet?' Susan asked trying to remember his name.

'Yeah, Wilfred Owen,' Tammy answered.

'But it's a long piece of music?' Susan remembered.

'We're only going to dance to the fourth part, the *'Dies illa, dies irae'* – it's the main climax.'

'OK...But,' Susan said hesitantly, 'you know, you'll probably be arrested again?'

'Why should they arrest us for dancing to the tourists in Strafalgar Square? Loads of street artists perform here.' Paula stated with some defiance. Then again she looked at Susan with those beautiful, serious eyes framed by her black jiba and said, 'But you promise to film everything? That, no matter what happens, you will keep filming to the very end? You promise?'

'Yes, I promise. But what do you want me to do with the recording?'

'If anything should happen, if we're arrested, we want you to upload the video to the Internet so that the world can see what's happening to women in this country. It will be a statement, a protest, like we said. But a protest no one sees is pointless. But a protest the whole world can watch may be worth it. I don't want to live in a society where the only way I can walk free and unmolested in the streets, is if I wear a patch announcing to every fuckwit I have VD.' Paula finished with obvious passion.

'You're right. So I should stand well back so that the MGs don't notice me.'

'Yes – if they see you they'll smash the camera and you'll be arrested. We're going to set up our stuff between the fountains down there,' Tammy pointed to a wide, flat space in-between the fountains that, even now, so early in the day, was thronging with people. Then she continued, 'We'll dance facing the steps to the national gallery. You should film from up here, away to one side, so that you're filming downwards – if you stand with the onlookers in the square they'll only get in the way. Paula – are you ready?'

Both women hugged each other and then Susan. Paula couldn't help repeating yet again 'You promise?' But Susan smiled and said there was no need to worry, she would do whatever it takes. They lifted their rucksacks onto the small wall, wriggled into the straps without exposing too much arm and set off down the steps into the square. Susan began filming.

Once they reached their chosen spot between the fountains, Susan filmed them helping each other take off their rucksacks. They stood them up, one leaning against the other, and Tammy began pulling wires and electronics from hers and setting up the speakers. Paula, however, began taking out from her rucksack what looked like heavy plastic bags and she walked a few paces away from Tammy and started emptying the contents onto the ground. When she had finished Paula had dumped about five or six piles of what looked like soaking wet clothes right around where they were standing. Then she began doing the oddest thing – she started pushing the wet clothes together to form a circle that completely enclosed them. Susan vaguely thought Paula must be marking out the area in which they were going to dance – because, she reasoned with herself, they probably needed quite a bit of space to move and twirl.

A few people stopped to watch what Paula and Tammy were doing but since nothing much was happening they moved on. Susan played with the zoom and filmed close-ups of Tammy setting up the amplifier and Paula forming the circle of wet clothes. Then she zoomed out to show the entire context of Strafalger Square with its famous lions and fountains.

Susan noticed her friends seemed ready. She adjusted the zoom getting the two women standing side by side in the centre of their circle. For a moment they appeared like two statues draped to the ground in black robes. Then Tammy and Paula lifted the front of their jibas, gave each other a quick kiss on the cheek, and Paula turned around and pressed something, presumably a play button. A few people stood to watch. The music started slowly but, even from where Susan was filming, it was loud and clear. More people came to watch the strange movements of the dance.

There was nothing smooth or poetic in the way Tammy and Paula moved. Rather the dance reflected the jerky, broken rhythms of the music. This was not music for classical ballet, instead the orchestra and choir seemed to demand the physical release of an energy centred on grief and inconsolable rage. As the music grew in volume and intensity so the crowd of spectators grew – each person seemed to be mesmerised both by the two dancing, fully-robed women and the seemingly chaotic music. Susan filmed on. She was glad she had remained at the top of the steps because the crowd below, watching the performance, was now becoming very large indeed.

Then Susan, looking through the camera's viewfinder, watched with disbelief as her two dancing friends simultaneously threw off their jibas at some wild crescendo in the music – the choreography was breath-taking.

'...Dies illa...dies irae...'

Some men in the crowd started pointing but they were in the minority and ignored because most of the spectators, male and female, were completely riveted by the performance. Not so the Morality Guardians. From somewhere outside the ring of onlookers, three MGs started pushing through the crowd towards Tammy and Paula. But when they reached the outer circle and were about to step across the line, suddenly a wall of flames six or seven feet high blazed upwards from the circle of clothes. Susan realised immediately they could not be wet with water but soaked with petrol. The MGs leapt back, one stamping his flaming foot. Tammy and Paula were now completely encircled by an impenetrable wall of fire.

'...dies irae...calamitatis et miseriae...'

Susan kept on filming. Many in the crowd at the front moved back away from the flames and intense heat. However, a minute later when some of the flames began to burn down, Susan couldn't see either of her two friends inside the ring of fire – they'd disappeared! But just as she thought the performance was over there was another dreadful, precipitous crescendo in the music and Tammy and Paula leapt up now dancing completely naked. They seemed to abandon the music and, instead of something choreographed, they embraced each other like lovers driven by passion. This was too much for the men spectators, not least the MGs – one of whom was trying to get a fire extinguisher working. The men started throwing shoes, books, anything they could hurl.

'...Libera me...Libera me...Libera me...'

Susan, whose heart was now almost bursting with fear, filmed on. The fire extinguisher sputtered to life. There was a small cloud of white smoke and then it seemed to go out. To penetrate the wall of flames two MGs started breaking the circle of burning clothes with their batons, but just as it seemed the show was over for the two women, they both climbed up onto their two rucksacks that were leaning together like a small step-ladder, and, when the music was at its most cataclysmic, Susan's two friends dowsed themselves in petrol, threw their arms tightly around one another and burst into a ghastly torrent of fire. At exactly this moment, the music – now at full volume – produced such a sudden frenzied detonation of emotion, such a truly gargantuan climax of anger and agony, of suffering and rage, it seemed that every atom of human suffering from the dawn of humanity to this very moment, was screaming across the face of the Earth like a wall of blistering pain. But the human torch of two women, clasped in a final embrace, was now beyond the reach of the living or the dead.

Although Susan tried to focus on her two friends being consumed, it was soon impossible, because their rucksacks, which must have been packed with containers of petrol, now exploded sending a massive inferno of yellow fire up into the sky. Whether it was the two women screaming or people in the crowd it was impossible to tell because everyone and everything seemed to be shrieking – even the towering column of flames that enveloped the two women seemed to be emitting a merciless screeching noise. The crowd, naturally, panicked and people began running in every conceivable direction just to get away from the grizzly scene....but, although her mind was reeling with indescribable anguish, and tears were rolling down her cheeks, still Susan kept on filming.

In the space of just a few seconds the music had reached an unbearable, wailing intensity so excruciating it felt as though every wretched act of inhumanity, all the hate humans had ever created, all the bitterness and violence they had ever celebrated, had been burnt, as a mark of shame, across the face of mankind. The useless moralities of violence, dominance, tyranny and oppression were finally going up in flames...or so it seemed.

*

The chauffeur stopped the car a mile from the city dump saying he was not permitted to enter the Untouchables' zone, so Rosie's father got out and started walking. After about ten minutes the familiar smell was all around him – the sweet odour of rotting garbage that had been his only 'fresh' air for decades. Now, strangely, he felt at odds wearing his new, clean clothes – what would the others think when they saw him dressed like a real city person? Would Helena be impressed or would she make fun of him? Would his children and the others tease him?

But all these thoughts were quickly dispelled when he saw the gulls. Something was not right – there were too many of them. Never in all the years he'd been living at the dump had the sky been so dark with seagulls, crows and – he stopped and gazed upwards –he could see several huge birds with enormous wingspans – vultures! He began running. He ran through what used to be the entrance and stopped – the mountains of bags, the shelters and tents, his people were all gone. There was nothing before him but an endless sea of broken, flattened rubbish bags. The wind blew pieces of paper and the odd plastic bag across the scene before him. There was not another human to be seen anywhere, no children, no Helena, nothing. He tried to work out what could have happened but the constant screaming of the birds as they circled looking for scraps made it all but impossible to think. He started leaping across the flattened bags shouting for his wife and children. In desperation he flung bags aside hoping to find some clue, some of trace of his people. Then he saw it. It was the small hand of a child severed at the wrist lying in the mud-print of a bulldozer's tracks. The bulldozers must have arrived and, without warning, levelled the mountainous heaps of rubbish together with the settlement – and its Roja people.

Rosie's father dropped down onto the broken bags and hammered the rubbish with his fists. He had been gone for less than a day and his world, his family, his friends had been wiped from the ground as though they had been dog dirt. And, even worse, he had given up his deepest joy – Rosie – to a stranger. He stood up slowly, tears falling from his eyes. In his grief he felt like an empty shell, something hollowed out and thrown away. Yet there was something he couldn't give up on.

It was getting dark. All this time he thought he was alone, but somewhere behind him he heard a noise and when he turned he caught sight of a man running between some bushes outside the dump gates. He called out 'Wait!', but when the man heard Rosie's father shout he stopped and hid behind a thick bush.

Rosie's father left the dump and walked slowly towards where the man was hiding. When he reached the bush he said quietly,

'What happened?'

The hiding man kept absolutely still and silent.

'It's me Josh, Josh Harrison. I won't harm you.' Rosie's father said.

The man slowly emerged and when he saw Rosie's father he asked anxiously and with some surprise,

'Josh!? You alone!?'

The man turned out to be one of Josh's neighbours. He told of how six machines had suddenly appeared like a wall of metal and crushed everything in their paths. The whole settlement had been covered and crushed with layer upon layer of rubbish bags.

'Did you see Helena!?' Rosie's father asked madly grabbing the man's arm. The man looked at him and with a face broken with sorrow replied,

'The woman what was expectin'?'

'Yes! Yes that's her! Did you see where she went!?'

The man didn't immediately reply he just nodded in the direction of the dump.

'Please! Have you seen her!?' Rosie's father repeated desperately.

' 'Cos her belly being so heavy, I guess she couldn't run like the rest.' he looked down at the ground and said almost in a whisper,

'I don't think she made it Josh. I saw her go down as the 'dozer pushed the bags over the tents. So sad Josh, so sad.'

Rosie's father let go of the man's arm and asked in a voice that showed he already knew the answer,

'And the others?'

The man shook his head and said nothing. For almost a minute both men remained in a thoughtless, stunned silence, then Rosie's father turned and gazed at the city before him. In all this world there was something he couldn't give up on, he did have one thing left, one anchor, one reason to breathe, one reason to live and fight. He started walking and then began to run towards the city.

'Joshua! Where you going!?' the man called out.

'To fetch my daughter!!' Rosie's father shouted to the darkening sky, 'I want my Rosie back!!'

*

It was a very delicate operation but, after two hours, it was going well. Rosie was under a general anaesthetic. Her small, delicate body was draped in the typical green gowns of surgery and, to prevent even the tiniest of movements, her head was fixed in position with a special clamp. The tumour was benign and in a relatively accessible part of Rosie's brain, and Professor Marshal was confident he could remove it completely and save Rosie's life. However, the operation required not only Professor Marshal's meticulous, steady hand, but also his infinite patience. Nothing could be done in haste. Nothing could be overlooked. Everything had to be done with superhuman care and precision. Because a child's brain and skull are not fully grown there is little space for surgical instruments, so one wrong move by the surgeon could result in catastrophe – permanent paralysis or death. The one nightmare the Professor needed to avoid at all costs was haemorrhage. Not only was sudden blood loss bad for the patient's brain, it obscured the surgeon's view of what he was doing. However, after two hours of intense concentration, the operation was proceeding smoothly and Professor Marshal and his team, were becoming more and more optimistic of a successful outcome. Then, for one fraction of a second, the sound of an odd commotion coming from the corridor outside the operation theatre, distracted the Professor's attention. The Professor stopped, looked up and frowned. But just as he was about to continue, the doors to the operating theatre suddenly burst open and three Blue Priests entered chanting –

'NaYa! Malus spicatum et nostrum verdammt! Malus spicatum et nostrum verdammt!!'

'Christ!! I don't believe this!! Get these fucking lunatics out of here!!!' Professor Marshal screamed, 'Call security!!'

'She needs to be sprinkled and purified with Blessed Blue Urine!'

'You need to collide with a dose of sanity!' the Professor shouted from behind his surgeon's mask, 'Get out of here! Now!' but the Professor's words had no effect because the priests started sprinkling a brown powder around the operating table on which Rosie lay, and then another four Blue Priests came through the doors singing, dancing and guiding a little Blue Dog on a lead.

'Sweet Mary! There's a hole in her head!' one of the Blue Priests exclaimed as he leant over the Professor's shoulder to look at Rosie's exposed brain, 'She'll lose her spirit!'

'You'll lose your fucking balls if you don't get out of my operating theatre!' threatened the Professor pointing his scalpel at the priest.

'Holy Blue Dogs ! You're right! Her head's open!' another blue priest shouted as he took a peep.

'It's brain surgery! You fool! What did you expect - a melon!?'

'There's blood everywhere!' exclaimed another priest who'd come to look.

'Wow! You don't say! Get out! OUT! I don't believe this! Get that filthy mutt out of here! For god's sake someone call security!'

'She must wear a jiba! Her demons will get out!' cried one of the priests.

'My demons will fry your fucking nipples if you bastards don't get the hell out of here!!! Quick! Before I lose it!!' the Professor raged.

'But we're exorcists!' shouted two of the Blue Priests into the Professor's face.

'No you're not! You're a bunch of raving screwballs!' the Professor screamed back, 'Now GO!!'

'We can't go until she is cleansed! Malus spicatum et nostrum verdammt!' chanted the priests.

'Holy fuck! I'll go mad!' shouted the Professor waving his scalpel in the air. At his feet the Blue Dog yapped with excitement. Then the Professor had a flash of inspiration. He grabbed the lead holding the little Blue Dog and sliced through it with his scalpel. He then quickly snatched the sacred mutt from the floor, ran out of the operating theatre and down the corridor with the dog under his arm squealing with fright.

'The bastard's stolen little Bluey! Quick!' one of the priests shouted.

The effect was immediate and just what Professor Marshal had hoped for – the six or so priests came running like madmen out of the operating theatre, their blue robes flapping, and sprinted down the corridor after their squealing demi-god. But Professor Marshal, still in his surgeon's apron, his mask and green hat, had reached a dead end.

In front of him were two lift doors. He hit the buttons and by incredible good fortune a lift stopped almost immediately. The doors slid open. Inside were several people. Behind him the Professor could feel and hear the pounding feet and screams of the blue priests. Acting on sheer impulse he threw the blue dog into the arms of a woman in the lift, jumped in and hit the down button.

As the doors slowly closed he couldn't help a cheeky wave at the blue priests as they vainly tried to throw themselves at the closing metal doors. The operating theatre was on the tenth floor and the lift move swiftly downwards. When it reached the sixth floor Professor Marshal got out leaving the blue, holy canine in the woman's arms. As the doors closed he told her it was a hygiene security risk and needed a home. He then walked towards the emergency stairs, but when he entered the concrete stair-well, above him he heard the echoing, frantic shouts and banging feet of the Blue Priests as they hurled themselves down the stairs above him trying to chase after the lift. Quickly Professor Marshal returned onto the sixth floor and hid behind a door with a small glass window with a view onto the stair-well. Keeping out of sight, he waited until the shouting and commotion on the stairs had passed – which meant, of course, the priests were now far below the sixth floor. He then climbed the stairs and returned to the operating theatre.

Fortunately his team had cleaned up the mess and brown powder and restored some calm and order. The Professor was acutely concerned about finishing Rosie's operation. To ensure he was as sterile as possible he had to 'scrub up' again, especially after handling the blue dog. But as he approached the operating table the anaesthetist said in a hushed, concerned voice that he was worried about Rosie's breathing as it had become erratic. Professor Marshal ordered the doors to the theatre to be locked and set to work immediately. He was in a position no neurosurgeon welcomed – he had to act fast.

*

When the first emergency vehicles arrived Susan stopped filming. She discreetly put her camera away and left the scene. Totally traumatised and shaken she walked back towards Bicester tube station unable to get the images she had recorded out of her head. Tammy and Paula must have intended all of this – why else would they have taken so many risks? Why else would they, at the end, have danced naked knowing the consequences? They had obviously rehearsed everything – even their final immolation by fire. Susan had promised not to let their 'protest' go unnoticed. Hard though it was – in her state of shock – to stop her feelings and thoughts from colliding, Susan resolved to return home immediately and play her part in her friends' sacrificial protest.

Taking the tube and a green female-only bus, it took Susan over an hour to reach her front door. Once inside she took out the camera, placed it at the centre of the kitchen table and sat down. She looked at the camera. This shiny, passive, black piece of super technology contained a record of something that could prove to be a momentous event in history. And yet if she did nothing this record would remain inside the polished black case and her life, and the lives of countless women, would continue on and on, as though nothing had happened. Should she do this? What could happen? She knew the answer to that question very well. If she uploaded the footage it would undoubtedly go viral within minutes, then it would be less than an hour before the security services and MGs burst into her flat. But if she didn't, she knew she would have to live the rest of her life feeling she was only half a human being – with a camera full of guilt hanging around her neck. She decided – for Tammy and Paula's sakes and for all the women who, like herself, were trapped by the iron bars going through men's heads – that she must do it. But first she had to prepare her escape. She packed a small rucksack with some clothes and essentials, and a small valise with more of her personal things she didn't want to lose. Only when she was ready to leave did she turn on her computer and connect the camera.

She used a special piece of software she had mastered when she'd worked for that awful online news agency – it was software that could upload a video to all the online social media channels simultaneously – so that you didn't have to do fifty individual uploads to the fifty or so social media sites. In less than 40 seconds the upload was complete. She had done it. She switched off her computer hoping this might delay her detection and placed the camera back at the centre of the kitchen table. Susan put a thick jumper over what she was already wearing and then over that her full-length durka. She pulled her jiba down hard and stuck the purple and yellow 'honour' patch to her arm. She was ready. Slinging her rucksack over her shoulder, Susan picked up her valise and left. She was a woman with only one thing visible to the world – venereal disease. She was a woman with every other aspect of her humanity invisible to the world, but not, fortunately, to herself – which is what mattered.

She set off and took a double-decker bus into town. On these types of buses women were not allowed on top so Susan sat alone downstairs looking through the bus window at the passing shops. The journey would be long but her train didn't leave Waterhoo for another three hours, so there would be plenty of time for her to be alone with her thoughts. Despite the images of the passing cars and shops in her eyes, in her mind she saw nothing but fire. Trying desperately to think of something else, Susan wondered if her Auntie Jane had received her letter. Auntie Jane had no computer or phone or internet access, so Susan had been forced to write an old-fashioned letter explaining her decision to leave the city. But since there had not been time for a reply to reach her, Susan realised she was going with blind hope that her auntie was willing to let her stay and help on the farm.

After about half an hour the bus became stuck at some traffic lights in a busy shopping area. Susan glanced at the advertisements in a supermarket window and thought she noticed a larger than normal reflection of herself in the glass. She turned her head and looked through the windows on the other side of the bus. There, in a home movie shop, were half a dozen vast cinema screens facing the street each with an enormous picture of Susan's face. Beneath her face were the words 'SUSAN McALLISTER – TERRORIST'. She was so shocked she impulsively stood up and got off at the next stop. She had intended to walk back to look again in the home movie window, but there was no need because in the window of a newsagents Susan's face was staring out on another huge screen. The newsfeed below said she was the suspected ringleader of a terrorist attack in Strafalgar Square earlier that day in which several innocent people had been killed. It went on to say she was a leading member of the godless, ultra-militant FRB (Feminist Resistance Brigade) which had been responsible for many terrorist incidents over the years. She was not to be approached because she was a fanatical lesbian, uncircumcised, dangerous and armed.

Susan stood transfixed – not so much by the sight of her name and face on every TV screen in the street, but more by the scale of the lies, by the injustice, by how crass and openly bloodthirsty it all was. She was now the prey. But how could they find her? So long as she wore her jiba she was safe? Not so. The newsfeed beneath her face on the screen now read that under the new Anti-Terrorism Legislation, the Police and Morality Guardians had the power to order any suspected female to remove her jiba to check her identity. To illustrate the point Susan's face disappeared and the screen showed police and MGs lifting women's jibas at Heathbow Airport. Then some sports item flashed over the screens. Susan looked away, numb inside, and started walking randomly down the street. However, some instinct of self-preservation stopped her and made her quickly collect her thoughts. She returned to the bus stop now even more determined to get out of the city.

But she needed to think. There could now be no question of her travelling by train or coach. She could not return to her flat. Also her friend's places would be watched. Even if she could afford to, she could not take a taxi or check-in to a hotel. She was by herself on the city streets, nowhere to go, with the entire security apparatus of a vast metropolis searching for her. Fortunately it was summer, so it did not begin to get dark until quite late, around 9pm, and curfew for women didn't begin until 10pm. She had therefore about six hours of liberty left – but Susan was determined they would not be her last six hours of freedom.

*

Rosie's father had a two hour car journey before him – if he had a car. As he was on foot, he had before him a journey of at least six hours, and it was getting dark. Not only was night approaching but he hadn't eaten for what seemed like days and he was ravenous. If he was to return on foot all the way to Farley Street, he needed to eat.

After running, jogging and walking for half an hour, he stopped to get his breath back. He was now in a residential district. He argued with himself that there was no point in continuing on deeper into the city because, even if he got to Dr. Abdulla-Smith's surgery by midnight, it would be closed. It made more sense to find something to eat now and then look for a place to sleep. In the morning he would be rested and ready to make a fresh start.

Fortunately his life of survival on the refuse dump had taught him exactly what to do. He found a busy restaurant and went to the rear. Just as he thought – outside the back door were several food bins into which uneaten food was being scraped roughly every ten minutes. Rosie's father waited until the dish scraper had gone and helped himself. Surprisingly some of the left-overs were still warm. However, because the food was incredibly spicy, after he'd eaten to his heart's content, he needed to drink some water, so he went into the outside toilet meant for the restaurant staff. The only available fresh water was down in the bowl of the toilet, so Rosie's father flushed the loo and captured the gushing water into a tin can he'd found in one of the food bins. No longer hungry or thirsty, he now needed to sleep. He fetched some cardboard boxes which he's seen stacked at the back of another shop, found an unlit doorway for shelter and quickly made a makeshift sleeping-bag by fitting several boxes end-to-end. He then wriggled inside, closed the two ends to keep out rats, and fell asleep.

When sleeping rough, if you wanted to attract no attention from the police, Rosie's father knew he had to be up and gone before sunrise. So, when the grey light of dawn glimmered through the cracks in his cardboard sleeping bag, he got up immediately. He again availed himself of the restaurant's outside toilet, returned the rather flattened boxes and set off towards the city's heart with one over-riding desire – to get to Rosie, no matter what the cost, to keep her safe from the good doctor, no matter what might happen.

Even this early the traffic had started to build. Because he guessed he still had at least another five hour journey ahead of him on foot, he began to search for some way to get a ride. Since he had no money, buses and trains were useless, so he began walking and hitching at the same time. But in his new shirt and trousers he didn't fit the down-and-out stereotype, he looked much too suspicious, much too respectable to be hitch-hiking, so nobody stopped.

Suddenly he saw the very thing. Lying on its side under a tree was what looked like an abandoned bicycle. The rear tyre was flat. He stood it up. It was unlocked and fairly new, it just looked crappy because it was covered in dirt from having been left beside the busy road. Rosie's father saw a petrol station on the next corner, so he wheeled the bike to the compressed air line. He blasted the rear valve with air and it worked – the tyre inflated to a good pressure and so instantly he set off before the punctured tyre flattened, but to his surprise and good luck it remained inflated.

Two hours later Rosie's father was cycling down Farley Street. It took him several minutes to recognise Dr. Abdulla-Smith's surgery as he had no idea of the number. He went up the steps knocked and rang. Jones answered .

'Ah, Mr. Harrison,' he said in a flat voice, 'Please, come in.'

'Rosie? How's my Rosie?'

'I'm afraid Dr Abdulla-Smith is away at a conference until tomorrow,' Jones replied not answering the question.

'Where is Rosie? I've made my decision. She will stay with me. We have only each other now.'

'Please come in to the lounge. Would you like something to drink? Some tea?'

'Yes...Yes that would be nice thank you,' replied Rosie's father following Jones into the lounge and siting down on the leather sofa. He continued, 'I've thought it over. I couldn't ask Helena. I've ….I've lost her, but I know if she were here she would agree with me, that Rosie belongs with her family…what's left of it.'

'Listen, Mr. Harrison,' Jones said soberly, 'There were complications.'

'Complications? What complications?' Rosie's father asked with a worried voice.

'I'm afraid…Rosie never made it. It was something to do with her breathing. She died towards the end of the operation.'

'NO!' screamed Rosie's father as the bitterest grief known to man burst from his heart. He slid off the sofa onto his knees and hammered the floor with his fists shouting over and over 'NO! NO! IT'S NOT TRUE!'

'Mr. Harrison! Please! I'm awfully sorry,' exclaimed Jones standing up in alarm. For several minutes Rosie's father was inconsolable – he cried and raged and hit his head with clenched fists. In the space of just forty eight hours his whole world and will to live had crumbled. He felt that life – especially his life – was nothing but a pointless charade that danced mockingly between poverty and death. What was the point of Rosie? What was the point of Helena? What was the point of himself? It all made no sense. Everything was pointless, meaningless trash, a rubbish tip of reproduction, hunger and injustice. Rosie was gone and she had taken his heart with her to the grave.

Half an hour later when Rosie's father seemed a little calmer, Jones offered to take him in the car to St. Mary's to say his last farewell to Rosie. Emotionally shaken into a bitter, bitter silence, Rosie's father just stood up and followed Jones out to the waiting car. Life was not life without his darling Rosie.

*

Cat and mouse. To Susan the city was beginning to feel like a cat. But, fortunately for her, this cat hadn't yet spotted the mouse, and anyway, this mouse looked the same as millions and millions of other mice. Susan had to travel right across the city to the south. They were looking for a woman, so they would naturally target the green, women-only buses, so she abandoned waiting at the bus stop and moved on. There was now only one option – she had to walk. How far she could get in six hours she didn't know. But if she walked and always mingled with the crowds of other women in their durkas, she would be relatively safe. She had only to remain an inconspicuous non-entity. What she would do when darkness eventually came, and she was a lone woman on the streets, she pushed far from her mind.

After tramping the city streets for almost five hours, Susan was exhausted. Tired though she was, she had made good progress and was well on her way along one of the main routes through the south of the city. But what was now beginning to worry her was the gathering twilight. It had begun sooner than she'd expected and she had already noticed a thinning of the number of women out on the streets. However, in this suburban labyrinth of houses and shops there was nowhere to go, no alternative but to push on into the growing dark. She kept telling herself naively that around the next corner there would be the obvious answer to where she could spend the night – a B&B, a boarding house, a hostel, a refuge for the homeless, a church hall, anything as long as she could rest and sleep. The first curfew patrol sped passed her but they didn't even glance in her direction. The situation was becoming critical. She couldn't risk being stopped, but, as the streets emptied of more and more women, that risk was growing. And now she was becoming conspicuous – a woman, alone, in a hurry, wearing a rucksack and carrying a valise – clearly she wasn't a mother or wife doing a little late shopping – she now stood out as a traveller.

She walked on for another half hour. By now the street lights had come on and it was getting seriously dark. In the distance coming towards her Susan made out another patrol car – however, you couldn't always be sure because often they used unmarked cars. But her fears were confirmed because as the car approached it began to slow down. Susan's heart began pounding. Without moving her head she glanced sideways and saw they were looking at her, but fortunately it was their tactic to slow down beside a woman who, they thought, was hurrying home for curfew. They accelerated away screeching their tyres in a show of dumb intimidation. Susan quickened her pace knowing they would soon turn around and come back to check if she was off the streets.

Susan came to a corner and down one poorly lit side street there seemed to be a patch of blackness where there were no houses. She headed straight for the dark gap. As she came near she saw it was a very small park with a clump of trees almost bordering the road. Without hesitating she walked behind the first tree and vanished into its black shadow. It was not a moment too soon – a patrol car turned into the street, its headlights slicing the darkness. Slowly it cruised passed where Susan was hiding. Seeing nothing the car turned around and accelerated back towards the bright main road. That was far too close. Now what was she going to do? So many desperate possibilities bombarded her mind Susan couldn't think straight. But instinctively she knew that when you're desperate it is so, so easy to make a stupid decision. Should she spend the night here? What if it rained? Should she risk walking on down the back streets? Should she knock at a door and ask for help? Or maybe, if she kept going, she could hide behind parked cars if any curfew police showed? She looked out from behind the tree up towards the main thoroughfare – everything seemed quiet.

'Have they gone?' a voice asked out of the darkness behind Susan.

'Who's that!?' Susan whispered loudly as she spun around terrified she'd been caught.

'Don't worry – I'm not one of those entrapment bastards,' a woman's voice replied.

'Then why are you hiding in the park?' Susan asked suspiciously.

'I'm guessing, the same reason you are,' the woman answered.

From behind a nearby tree a woman, wearing a full durka, separated from the tree's deep shadow and came a little closer to Susan. Susan backed away slightly.

'What do you want? I've no money,' Susan said gripping her valise tighter.

'Neither have I. Where are you going?' the woman asked quietly.

'I'm going south, but I'm lost. I got caught by the curfew. I don't want to be picked up by the police. One of their patrol cars had started following me, so I came in here to hide.'

'Like me,' the woman replied.

'But why are you breaking curfew?' asked Susan.

'Now you sound like the fucking Morality Police – sorry, I just can't stand this shit I have to go through every time I leave my house. Makes me sick. I only live down the street and I don't see why I have to hide in the dark like an animal just to see some friends. Why don't you come with, they'd love to see a new face – it's not far,' the woman suggested in a friendly way. Here was a chance Susan thought, but was she thinking clearly? Who was this strange woman?

'I...I can't – I've got to get going,' Susan replied even though inside she was shouting 'yes! yes! please help me!'

'In the dark? Baby you won't get a mile before they pick you up and throw you behind bars – or worse,' said the woman stepping a little closer to Susan. The woman slowly reached out and touched Susan gently on the arm and said,

'Don't worry. I know it must seem crazy meeting in the dark like this, but we're both hiding from the same bastards. Come with, you can trust me – and, if you don't like my friends, you can just leave, go on your way, no one will stop you,' the woman said quietly. She moved closer. Her hand gently lifted the lower half of Susan's jiba and she whispered, 'Such a pretty mouth.'

'I...I...' Susan began.

'Sssshh...' the woman replied putting her finger over Susan's lips and she lifted her own jiba and softly kissed Susan. It was not a forced, far-too-eager kiss – it was gentle, warm and clearly sexual, a kiss that Susan – to her own surprise – responded to. The woman touched her breast but Susan did not recoil.

'There – friends at last,' the woman said tenderly when they'd finished and she asked, 'How old are you?'

'Twenty three. What about you?' Susan responded.

'Almost thirty. Come, let me carry your bag,' the woman offered.

'Where are we going?' Susan asked.

'To some friends – it's all hush-hush – just around the corner. Come on, give me your bag, it looks heavy.'

 'Are you a thief?' Susan asked in a cheeky, unsure way.

'I am – I steal young women from the streets at night and seduce them,' the woman responded in an equally cheeky manner.

'Well, I'll have to consider myself stolen,' Susan replied smiling behind her jiba as she handed the woman her bag.

'Take my hand,' the woman said reaching out her hand for Susan to hold.

'But I don't even know your name,' Susan objected.

'I know – isn't it delicious?' the woman answered mischievously. Susan took hold of the woman's hand and gave her name.

'Susan.'

'Samantha ...Sam.'

'I'm not sure about this – you might murder me, chop me up and sell me as sausage meat,' Susan said with cautious sarcasm.

'I might. Because, from what I've tasted, you're quite yummy – so I might eat you myself. The last woman I cooked was so tough and chewy,' Sam replied playfully and she continued, 'O come on, lighten up, how do I know you won't dine on me? But I *am* inviting you to my table,' Sam finished and she pressed herself against Susan and kissed her again. Then, breaking their embrace, Sam said in a serious voice,

'Come on, we must go before those bastards come back. It isn't safe for us to be out like this. Give me your hand and stay close.'

Making sure the road was empty they both ran across the street and vanished down an unlit alleyway. After more turns they arrived at what looked like a row of identical, lock-up garages – only it was difficult to tell what they were because of the dark. Sam knocked on something metallic and a small door opened. Instantly the sound of jazz music and laughter filled the darkness.

Sam quickly pulled Susan through the doorway into what was a vestibule for clothes. Immediately Sam threw her jiba onto a table and asked Susan to help her pull off the durka. Underneath Sam was wearing tight black trousers and a bright red jacket open at the front – she looked so beautiful Susan thought.

'Now yours,' Sam urged, but Susan, who couldn't risk being recognised, backed off and said she just felt very shy – especially as she wasn't wearing any special gear, just her drab old clothes. Sam didn't, of course, want to frighten Susan into leaving so soon, so she just shrugged her shoulders, took Susan's hand and pulled her into what was a vivacious, brilliant, sparkling other world – men and women dancing together! Men and women eating and drinking together at the same tables! Women wearing short skirts! Men wearing short skirts! Women kissing women! Men kissing men! Even men discreetly kissing women! And every one was having such fun!

Sam waved to some of her friends and brought Susan over to say hello. Standing there in her full length black durka and a jiba covering her head and face, Susan felt the full stupidity of her situation. But there was nothing she could do. She so much wanted to throw off her covering and join the party, but it was just too risky. She looked like a Ring Wraith standing amidst the most happy, carefree and colourful people in the world.

Then she noticed something strange had begun happening – all the people at the tables and on the dance floor had turned in Susan's direction and had started rhythmically clapping and chanting -

> There's no disgrace
> To show your face!
> There's nothing vile
> In a lovely smile!

Sam looked at Susan's anxious eyes in the window of her jiba. She put her arms around Susan to encourage her and whispered,

'No one cares about your clothes – they're just trying to be friendly. Come on, let them see you. *I* want to see you.' Sam finished, gently squeezing Susan's hand. The chanting continued and became louder. Slowly Susan began to remove her jiba. People started cheering and shouting encouragement. When she finally pulled it free, she defiantly tossed it into the air, expecting everyone to cheer wildly.

But almost instantly every person went silent. The music played on for about ten seconds then stopped. Then someone said audibly,

'It's her!'

Susan stood and tried to smile but inside she was burning up with shame and fear. How could she have been so stupid? Now what? Sam put her hand on Susan's shoulder and said quietly, 'You're the woman they're looking for.' Susan just nodded her head. Sam stroked her cheek. Susan stared into Sam's beautiful eyes and explained, 'They want me for uploading the video of what happened this morning.'

A woman came over and stood in front of Susan and stared long and hard into her face. Then, giving her a huge hug, the woman loudly declared,

'Don't you worry hen – so long as I have breath left in ma body those bastards will never find you! You did the right thing! You did the right thing for all of us! What happened was dreadful, but the world needs to know! The world needs to know what we're going through here! Baby, you're a fucking heroin!!'

The crowd of silent people broke into spontaneous cheers and applause and they came and surrounded Susan, patting her on the back and telling her how courageous she was. After several minutes of reassuring Susan that she was among friends – all of whom understood and supported what she had done – the music started up again and people began to relax and return to their tables. Many, however, couldn't take their eyes off the 'heroin' in their midst and when they caught Susan's attention they waved and blew kisses.

Sam came over and sat close to Susan. She lent her head on Susan's shoulder and said quietly,

'You poor thing, no wonder you were so frightened. I'm going to have to take good care of you. Do you like cats?'

'Can I stay at your place for a while?' Susan asked a little unsure.

'I stole you off the streets remember,' Sam replied with a smile and she caressed Susan's thigh and added, 'Come, let's go home – one of the guys has offered to give us a lift.'

'Sam?'

'What?'

By way of reply Susan lent forward, kissed Sam on the cheek and whispered, 'Thank you.'

*

Dr. Abdulla-Smith's 'conference' was only with one other person – Professor Marshal. They sat in the Professor's office in St. Mary's and neither seemed in the mood to talk. Eventually Dr. Abdulla-Smith broke the awkward silence,

'Well Henry, I suppose we'd better get this ghastly business sorted.'

The Professor sighed and with a flat voice related the medical facts,

'Sub-dural haemorrhage of a major basal vessel supplying the occipital cortex. Her breathing became erratic and the pulse started to become asymmetric.'

'Hummm a great pity Henry, but I suppose these details are now irrelevant. If you can just sign the release documents I'll arrange for the body to be taken to my private morgue,' Doctor Abdulla-Smith said disappointed.

'I'm sorry Shazaad I can't do that,' Professor Marshal replied.

'Why not this time!?' the Doctor asked clearly irritated and he continued, 'Henry, I'm beginning to get the distinct feeling you're purposely blocking our work.'

'Not at all,' the Professor objected.

'The last time this happened, you said the corpse was sent to the wrong morgue. And the time before that you said MI6 arrived with a dead-or-alive extradition order. Really Henry, unless you can come up with an adequate reason why you can't sign the release documents this time, I'll have to refer you to The Temple and let them deal with you,' the Doctor concluded obviously exasperated.

'I can't sign them Shazaad – the body was sent to the bio-hazard incinerator this morning. You can always have the ashes.'

'The incinerator!? What on earth for? The ashes are worthless, you know that!' Dr. Abdulla-Smith cried getting more frustrated.

'They'd make good fertiliser,' humoured the Professor.

'Henry this is no time for jokes! I admire the Inglish eccentric sense of humour, but there's a time and a place. Couldn't we at least harvest her eyes? Even with one viable eyeball we could re-coup at least $20,000.'

'I'm sorry, it's completely out of the question,' Professor Marshal said firmly and he went on, 'Remember, you sent the patient here as an emergency so there was no time for a blood test. We did the test post op, and what we found was devastating – she was crawling alive with the most virulent strain of MRSA we have ever detected. I'm sorry Shazaad but the infection was total.'

'If only she hadn't been an Untouchable she might not have been so infected,' the good Doctor sighed dejectedly.

'Well you did take that risk Shazaad. You knew her background – she was a Roja?'

'What about harvesting her ovaries? The ova would still be viable and they could be frozen and sole separately for at least $15,000 each. And with the number of eggs in a juvenile ovary we could be talking of something in excess of $100,000 Henry – isn't it at least worth a try?'

'I'm afraid Shazaad – ' but the Doctor cut across the Professor saying,

'Also the market for bone marrow is particularly buoyant at the moment,' the Doctor said hopefully.

'Shazaad, I can't agree to any of this. The MRSA bacteria we found was not just potent, but, worst of all, it was a completely unknown strain. You need to understand Shazaad there is not a single antibiotic on the entire planet that can kill or control it. The risks of this getting out are beyond a nightmare – because of it we've already had to incinerate half the operating theatre and its equipment. Of course, your Blue Dog lunatics who interrupted the surgery didn't help – you need to rein them in. An operating theatre is no place for superstitious claptrap Shazaad. It's got to stop.'

'I disagree Henry – if there is any place the intervention of the divine is sorely needed it's during surgery.'

'What are you a scientist or a priest?' the Professor asked as though pushing a needle into the good Doctor.

'I'm not sure they are so different,' the Doctor commented dismissively.

'Oh but they are – they couldn't be more different,' Professor Marshal replied decisively. Then softening his voice he said, 'But listen, now's not the time to get into a discussion of metaphysics. I'm going to make you a generous offer Shazaad: I will forget passing on to you the considerable costs of this operation – costs that include, I might add, the total refurbishment and sterilisation of the operating theatre – if you get the Blue Dog crackpots off my back? Do we have a deal?'

Doctor Abdulla-Smith was silent. There was a frown on his brow. Eventually he stood up to leave, saying,

'Henry, I know many surgeons who have an excellent understanding of the necessity of organ transplants and who are more than willing to assist The Temple in its charity work. But with you I have the uncanny intuition that you just don't – or won't – understand. I'll see what I can do – but this time it will not be easy. The Temple is becoming increasingly concerned about this lack of co-operation. I'll see myself out. Goodbye.'

The good Doctor left and the Professor sighed with relief – he'd managed to get away with it again.

Dr. Abdulla-Smith walked to the lift but as he stood waiting his phone buzzed. It was Jones.

'Ah, where is he now?' the Doctor asked and continued, 'Just take him to reception in the main entrance and leave him there, they'll tell him where to go – we've done enough. And Jones – meet me in five minutes outside A & E...I've a little job for you.'

Dr. Abdulla-Smith put away his phone. He changed his mind about taking the lift and, instead, took the stairs down. When he reached the first floor he made his way along a corridor in the direction of the A & E department, which was, conveniently, in the opposite direction to the main entrance.

Outside A & E he met Jones. They walked to the hospital car park, found the car and got in.

'He thinks he can fool me,' the Doctor said as he took out some papers from a briefcase. He pulled out a tray and smoothed one of the sheets flat. Then he took a pen and wrote along some dotted lines 'Family requests immediate burial for religious reasons, do not cremate.' Dr. Abdulla-Smith then signed along a dotted line at the bottom 'Professor H. Marshal'.

'Sir!?' Jones said surprised.

'Don't worry Jones, I've been practising. Marshal has signed many documents of ours in the past, his signature won't have changed all that much – despite his dotage!'

Jones just raised his eyebrows and said nothing. The good Doctor now gave his instructions,

'Take these release documents to the hospital incinerator – '

'Is this for the girl's body?' Jones interrupted.

'No, no, we're too late for that, Marshal cremated her this morning. No, you will have to fill in the name of one of the bodies waiting for cremation. There will be the usual name tag around the big toe. Be discreet. Just get the name of the deceased and write it in here. I don't intend to disappoint The Temple again.'

The Doctor pointed out where in the document Jones should fill in the name of the dead person. Jones then asked,

'Any preference Sir? Male or female?'

'What did we get last time? It was a male wasn't it. Try and make it a female this time – youngish if you can – the organs will be in better condition. I'll call Baker and get him to bring over the hearse and meet you in the car park near the incinerator. When you get back to the surgery remember to put it straight into the freezer – we don't want any smelly accidents like last time. Good luck.'

*

'You wish to see Professor Marshal?' the hospital receptionist asked surprised.

'Yes.' Rosie's father replied. He was still in a state of numb shock and the thought of him saying a last farewell to Rosie as she lay white and lifeless on some hospital stretcher, made him feel even worse. Could he really go through with this? He knew that seeing the very last remnant of his former joy and love, lying before him dead and cold, would be an experience so miserable it would never leave him until his own dying day – and maybe not even then. But he still loved Rosie too much to just walk through the exit doors in the hospital, to leave and never to have said one last goodbye.

'Professor Marshal's a very busy man, I'll just see if he's in his office.' The receptionist pressed a button and tried to smile at the rather sad-looking gentleman before her.

'Hello? Professor Marshal? I have a Mr. Harrison in reception. He says you operated on his daughter Rosie?...Yes...Yes of course, not a problem Professor, thank you.' Putting down her phone she smiled at Rosie's father and said,

'Well, you're in luck. Professor Marshal's not operating today. He'll see you now. If you just wait a moment I'll get someone to show you the way.'

After a couple of minutes an orderly arrived and took Rosie's father in the lift and up to Professor Marshal's office on the tenth floor. The orderly knocked and the Professor welcomed Rosie's father into his office, immediately shaking his hand and offering him a chair.

'Please, please, sit down Mr. Harrison, I'm so happy to meet you. Now I know you must have a lot of questions concerning Rosie's operation,' the Professor began.

'I only want to know if she suffered?' Rosie's father asked sadly.

'No! Not in the slightest!' the Professor replied enthusiastically, 'You have nothing to worry about Mr. Harrison, Rosie was under a general anaesthetic until the very end, she would have felt nothing. But before I talk about Rosie I would just like to ask you a few things first – if that's OK with you of course?

'Yes, it's...it's good.'

'I just want to clarify in my mind your connection to Dr. Abdulla-Smith – how did you meet him? How did you become involved in the Blue Temple and how did he become involved with you and Rosie?'

'It was all by chance really...'

Rosie's father then went on to describe exactly what had happened the day before in Farley Street, and how later, after Dr. Abdulla-Smith had called Professor Marshal to arrange the operation, he'd said he would pay for everything only if Rosie became his child bride.

'What!?' Professor Marshal declared, almost falling out of his chair, 'He said that!? He went so far? I can't believe it! It's despicable!

Listen, Mr. Harrison – I want you to promise me something very, very important. I want you to promise to have nothing more to do with either Dr. Abdulla-Smith or The Temple, either now or in the future. They exploit vulnerable people like yourself who are in sudden, dire need of medical help – I have tried working with them in the past, but, in my opinion, they are both disgusting organisations only pretending to do charity work. In reality, they are spreading the most detestable stupidity the world has ever seen.'

'But they said they would help?' Mr. Harrison replied innocently.

'I know – that's exactly what they seem to do, but the truth Mr. Harrison, I can assure you, is very different. But now,' the Professor suggested in a softer voice, 'let's talk about Rosie.'

'You said, she didn't have any pain, she didn't suffer?'

'Of course not – you see one of the strange things about neurosurgery is that the brain needs no anaesthetic because there are no nerves in the brain to register any trauma to the brain tissue itself – it's a fascinating area to work in.'

'So you mean Rosie couldn't have felt anything?'

'Exactly right.'

'But they told me there'd been 'complications'?And at the end she'd-'

'No!' interrupted the Professor, 'Whoever told you that was completely wrong Mr. Harrison – the only 'complications' we experienced were those idiotic priests who barged into the operating theatre shrieking demented nonsense during Rosie's operation. There were no complications at all. But, Mr. Harrison,' the Professor took a deep breath and said, 'I think it's now time.'

'For what?' asked Rosie's father, though he knew what was coming.

'I want you to prepare yourself for a shock,' the Professor responded.

Rosie's father realised that now had come the moment he had been dreading. The Professor stood up and said,

'Please Mr. Harrison come with me – as awful as you think this might be I can assure you there's no reason to be alarmed.'

Rosie's father stood up as though his own death sentence had just been past and he followed the Professor from his office out into the corridor. The Professor, however, seemed quite buoyant and chatty, but Rosie's father suspected it was probably just his way of trying to be polite and optimistic in the face of Rosie's death. They walked along several corridors and took some back stairs up to the very top floor of the hospital where it seemed unduly quiet. This must be where they keep the recently dead patients, Mr. Harrison thought – though it did seem an odd place because it was so airy and full of sunlight. They came to a locked door which the Professor opened with an impressive key and he remarked,

'Just in case.'

They went through and locked the door behind them, climbed some more stairs and came to a door at the end of a narrow passageway.

'After you Mr. Harrison,' the Professor said trying to hide a smile. Mr. Harrison went in and there in bed with her head in a bandage was Rosie as bright and as beautiful as ever!

'Rosie!!' shouted her father as he ran and almost threw himself onto Rosie's bed in his eagerness to embrace, kiss and hug her. But the Professor quickly intervened and said that Rosie was still in rather a delicate condition because her stitches were only just starting to heal and she could not be moved too quickly or hugged too hard. So instead, Rosie's father sank his head into the bedclothes and wept uncontrollably, and it was apparent to the Professor that it was he –

Mr. Harrison – who really needed the hugs and comfort. Through his muffled sobs he kept repeating, 'O Rosie! Rosie! They told me you was dead!'

The Professor put his hand on Mr. Harrison's shoulder and with a rather sombre voice said,

'I'm afraid that's my fault.'

'Don't cry daddy, I'm feeling much better. All those horrible lights have gone. I thought I'd woken up into a dream – and I've got books daddy, lots and lots of books – look!'

'She's right Mr. Harrison, no sooner did the anaesthetic wear off than she asked for a book to read! I was dumbfounded – the only thing I had handy was an old medical dictionary with 800 pages but Rosie devoured it in less than a couple of hours. Rosie has remarkable talents Mr. Harrison. Listen. Errr... Rosie what's *Meiboitis*?'

'That's easy peezy – it's when the glands in the eyelids are all inflamed because of an infection. But it's not fatal.' Rosie replied, her eyes sparkling at her new found knowledge.

'You see – she's a national treasure!' the Professor beamed.

'Come on daddy! I can teach you too if you want!'

The Professor left them to be alone together saying he would return shortly. Rosie's father eventually looked up from the bedclothes and, although he was still visibly shaken, it was possible to sense the indescribable joy beginning to overwhelm him.

'Rosie! You are so wonderful! It's so wonderful you're still alive!'

Rosie and her father spent about half an hour alone together before the Professor returned and asked if Mr. Harrison could come with him back to his office. It was, he said, important that Rosie rested and didn't become too over-excited. Professor Marshal then offered to let Mr. Harrison stay in a room adjoining Rosie's until, he said, she was ready to go home. Back downstairs the Professor closed his office door, drew up a chair next to Rosie's father and began,

'I'm afraid I owe you an apology Mr. Harrison. No doubt you are, quite rightly, wondering why Dr. Abdulla-Smith's assistant told you Rosie had died at the end of her operation. That was my fault entirely and I beg your pardon if it caused you any distress. I did this because I wanted Dr. Abdulla-Smith and his Blue Dog lunatics, to believe that Rosie had died and was therefore beyond their reach. A number of my colleagues and I have suspected for some time that this particular doctor, with the full support and knowledge of the Blue Dog Temple, somehow acquires – legally or illegally we don't know – newly deceased bodies and removes as many of the organs as he can, to sell on the open, and not-so-open market. This provides both the Doctor and the Temple with a considerable source of money – it's one of the reasons why they are so wealthy. They pretend they are saving peoples' lives by helping transplant surgery, but that's just a ruse, a ploy to hide something far more sinister. What this is we don't know. There have, of course, been lots of rumours but to be honest no one really knows the truth.' Professor Marshal paused, smiled and continued,

'Now, enough about the good Doctor and his Blue pals, let's come to the good news. I want you to know that Rosie's operation was a complete success and she should make a full recovery – with enough rest and books of course.'

The Professor went on to say that Rosie would probably need at least six weeks convalescence in either a hospital or some quiet facility in the countryside – what did Mr. Harrison have in mind? When Rosie's father explained the circumstances back 'home' the Professor looked very grave indeed. He couldn't stomach the thought of letting a gifted child like Rosie return 'home' to one of the city's dumps, to roam about eating left-overs from rubbish bags like some scavenging animal – if anything the risks if infection would be horrendous. When Rosie's father had finished describing what life was like back 'home', the Professor was quiet for some time. Eventually he stood up and said,

'Humm... I have an idea.'

*

Susan moved into Sam's place. To say they were in love would be a colossal understatement. It was as though they had both fallen off a cliff and were still falling. The joy and passion they showed in each other was obvious to anyone who saw them together, and sometimes it was so wonderfully exclusive, it was as though the rest of the world and the people in it, didn't exist. However, they couldn't really go out to the shops or for a walk or be seen together in public, because they simply couldn't refrain from holding hands, or walking arm-in-arm, and that would have alerted the MGs immediately. In some ways the claustrophobia of society outside, with all its rules and ordinances, forced the two women to seek in each other the liberation which the outside world denied them. As the days turned into weeks, Sam's and Susan's ardour for each other did not fade, instead it became deeper. A bond began to grow between the two women which, unbeknown to them, would become so strong it would change their lives forever.

Sam was a primary school teacher who worked part time in a local school. She loved kids and the crazy ways they saw the world about them. She had had a few partners over the years but never 'the' right one, until now. This relationship felt profoundly 'different' somehow – she couldn't explain it in words, it was like something written down in her viscera, some unspoken, raw commitment towards Susan she had never experienced before for anyone else.

However, while Sam was away teaching in the mornings, Susan had her mind on practical matters. She knew she needed to contact her aunt – Auntie Jane. So she wrote a brief, old-fashioned letter saying she had met someone and had decided to stay in the city for the time being, but would it be alright if they came to visit her on the farm? It was too risky to send the letter with Sam's address inside, so it was arranged for any replies to be sent to a friend's house where either she or Sam could pick them up. The system worked well and two weeks after sending her first letter, Susan received an astonishing reply –

Dear Susan,

You are so like your Mum! Always changing your mind! No worries – it would be lovely to see you again after – how long has it been? – almost 8 years! Please do come whenever you want. I don't go anywhere much these days 'cos my back's giving me trouble – you know I'm growing old like old Bonny – do you remember the horse old Bonny? He's still going. My lovely sheep dog Rexy died some months ago – I do miss her. Anyway let me get to the good news. Just over a month ago something terrible and wonderful happened. And it's made my life especially hard but at the same time so amazing I can't really believe it. No, I haven't won the lottery – it's something much better. What happened was, I went to bed early as usual – I was knackered after digging potatoes all day – and I was just about to fall asleep when I heard the most terrible screams of a woman coming from outside. I threw my dressing gown on and went out with the torch. The screams seemed to come and go and I could tell it was a woman in awful pain. But I couldn't see anything so I started looking first in the barn and then in the tool sheds. Then I opened the door to one shed and there on the floor was a woman covered in blood screaming. I saw straight away she was in labour and I tried to help but there was nothing I could do. The baby had got stuck somehow but because I've helped lots of animals give birth I must have done the right thing 'cos the baby suddenly slid out on to the floor. I cut the cord with some scissors and tied a knot. But the poor woman died almost as soon as the baby was out. There was blood everywhere. I guess she must have bled to death. But the baby was alive and it started crying – a good sign I guess. Well you can imagine how I felt on my own and all. But the baby needed attention so I wrapped it in a towel I got from the washroom and took it inside the house to keep it warm and clean it. The poor wee mite! You should have seen it Susan you would have cried! Anyway after I'd cleaned it and wrapped it up it fell asleep. I went back to the shed and it was an awful sight. The poor woman was as white as a ghost. Who was she? What was she doing here? I kept thinking. What was I going to do with her? I mean what do you do with someone who dies in your tool shed? Call the police? You know I'd never do that! The police are just bastards – excuse my language Susan but I think you know why – after the way they treated your uncle when he spoke out against those idiots in the Temple I'll never trust them again. Anyway, the next morning I decided to bury the poor woman in the peach orchard, in a nice spot, and keep the whole thing quiet. So here I am, a fifty year old widow with a beautiful wee baby daughter that's dropped out of the sky – and I still haven't given her a name! My neighbours live too far away to have heard anything so lord knows what they are going to think when they catch sight of the baby. Just as well some of the ewes are lambing 'cos so far I've been able to feed the wee thing on sheep's milk. So that's my awful and wonderful news. I still can't believe it. She's worth more to me than all the lotteries in the world! If you come for a visit it would be better to come and stay over the week end – that

way we'll have more time to catch up and say hello after 8 years!
Take care,

Lots of love,

     Auntie Jane.

Susan had read the letter to Sam on a Saturday morning when they were having a lie-in.

'Wow!' Sam said, 'She sounds amazing!'

Susan said nothing, she just stared at Sam over the top of the letter. Sam looked at Susan.

'What?' Sam asked puzzled.

Still Susan said nothing but kept looking at Sam with these big, yearning eyes.

'What?...What are you loo-...? Oh no.' Sam said shaking her head, 'You're not think-...? Susan, we...we can't.'

Susan lowered the letter and said quietly,

'You told me you loved kids. I could look after it while you're teaching – it would be perfect.'

'It'd never work Susan, we'd stand out a mile. And anyway...it's been banned.'

'Now *you* sound like the fucking Morality Police. Yes, it's been banned, I know that – which is all the more reason to try Sam, because the chance to have our own child will never exist – ever.'

'But Susan, we couldn't take it from your Auntie – she sounds like she really wants to keep it.'

'I'm not talking about taking it. But, don't forget, she's over fifty and trying to run a farm singlehanded – how can she look after a new-born baby as well? Let's go see! Please Sam! She sounds so sweet!'

'You're a broody bitch Susan – that's the real reason!' Sam teased.

'Your fault,' Susan teased back, 'every time you touch me you make me ovulate!'

The visit to Auntie Jane was arranged for the following weekend. Since women were no longer allowed to drive, Sam asked one of her male friends, Alex, if he would take them in his car if they paid for the petrol. It was agreed.

They didn't speak much about Auntie Jane's new baby for the rest of the week. But in Susan's mind it popped up every now and then like a tiny, precious ghost. In Sam's mind there was nothing but quiet amazement at what was beginning to happen to her life.

*

After a couple of weeks living secretly at the top of the hospital, Rosie and her father were coming down with a serious case of cabin fever. They had, of course, had their meals brought up by a trustworthy nurse and Rosie had had the dressing on her wound changed, but the Professor knew that, in an organisation as large and as complex as a hospital, it was only a matter of time before someone realised something clandestine was going on. He could sense that Rosie and her father were getting more and more restless by the day – and he didn't blame them – but it just seemed the safest option to keep them out of sight of the Blue Dog priests who, totally unannounced, would sometimes arrive at the hospital to 'purify' patients. However, it was only when one of his colleagues said, teasingly, that lately he had been acting strangely, that the Professor decided to act.

He took the lift as far as the twelfth floor and walked up the deserted back stairs, unlocked the door and went through. Rosie and her father were in Rosie's room. Rosie was sitting in bed surrounded by open books reading. Her father sat at a table by the window bent over, doing something with his hands. When the Professor entered they both looked up and smiled.

'Professor Marshal!' Rosie called out.

'Yes Rosie?'

'Did you know that if you stuck all the DNA in your body end to end it would stretch about five hundred thousand times around the Earth!'

'Did you know,' Professor Marshal responded, 'that last week a man in America, who had been hit on the head by a ball, woke up and found he could recite pi to 1000 decimal places.'

'I don't know which would be the worst headache!' Rosie laughed, then hardly stopping to take a breath she said, 'But you know Professor I've been thinking about haploid cells.'

'Oh really?' the Professor replied (inside he was thinking 'Oh dear what now?')

'Yes. You see I've found out that to get a fertilised diploid cell you need one female haploid cell to meet one male haploid cell – the male sperm cell fertilising the female egg cell.'

'Yeees...' the Professor mused wondering where on Earth this was going.

'Well that's the way it's always been, like how nature works. But I wondered what would happen if a female haploid cell could fertilise another, different, female haploid cell – like an egg from one woman fertilising the egg from another woman. Or you could even have one male sperm cell fertilising another, different, male sperm cell – wouldn't that be amazing Professor!? Do you think it's possible?'

'My word Rosie! I'm not sure I've done the right thing giving you all these medical books! To be honest Rosie I've never really thought about it that way – you certainly have a questioning mind – I think you're going to be a scientist one day.'

'But do you think it could work?' Rosie persisted.

'Well the normal way is for half the genetic information of the female (that's the female haploid cell) to combine with half the genetic information from the male (the male haploid cell) to produce a cell with all the genetic information to make a unique individual – a baby.

'Yes, that's right, but – '

'So what you're asking is, why can't the two halves that combine, both be female halves? Or the two halves both be male halves?'

'Exactly!' Rosie answered enthusiastically.

'Well, there is something called parthenogenisis where reproduction can happen without fertilisation – this is sometimes called asexual reproduction. But what you – I think – are talking about is a type of sexual reproduction that would happen between two cells of the same sex but different people? Hummm I'm not sure, Rosie, anyone has ever thought of it that way before. I certainly don't know the answer – though it is an intriguing possibility. So I guess you'll just have to research it.'

'Does that mean more books?' asked Rosie's father from the table.

'Perhaps. But listen you two, we've got to talk...'

The Professor began to explain how it was becoming too risky for them to stay hidden in the hospital, and he went on,

'About five or so years ago I bought an old barge that had been turned into a house boat by its previous owner. I had this fantasy of taking off into the quiet countryside at week-ends, just me and my wife, and we did for a while. But to be honest my interest has waned a bit and I've been thinking of selling it. Now – I think you can see where I'm going – I thought you and Rosie could live on the barge for a while, take care of it, or something like that? The canal where the barge is moored is only a couple of miles from my house. No one will find you there, you'll be safe and Rosie needn't go to school – that's the last thing we want.'

'Why's that?' Rosie's father asked.

'Because our schools are now just places of indoctrination – the kids spend hours reciting Blue Dog mumbo jumbo until their brains turn to jelly,' the Professor answered with some bitterness, then, more brightly, he asked, 'Anyway, what do you say?'

Of course, Rosie and her father didn't need any persuading – especially after being cooped up for two weeks in two small rooms – and the idea of living in a barge on a canal was just too exciting for words.

'That's wonderful!' beamed the Professor and he stood up to leave. But just as he passed Rosie's father the Professor caught sight of what Rosie's father had been busy doing.

'My word! But they're beautiful! Truly! Did you make them?'

'I've always kept myself busy with my hands,' Rosie's father replied with genuine modesty.

'But they're really stunning – completely unique – I've never seen anything like this. May I?' The Professor picked up a bracelet from the table where Rosie's father had been working and examined it with amazement.

'What's it made from?'

'I just use any old electrical wires. I take off the plastic coating and use the bright copper. Sometimes I use the silver-looking fuse wire just to add something different. But I get all the patterns out of my head.'

The Professor turned the bracelet over and was speechless at the exquisite, delicate intricacy of how the thin copper and silver wires had been perfectly braided together and then again interwoven with each other. The manual dexterity and patience to achieve this must have been phenomenal he thought.

'Mr. Harrison, could I possible buy one for my wife – she'll be absolutely stunned.'

'Professor, after all you have done for me and Rosie, your request is terrible. I would be honoured if you took it for you wife. The first one I ever made was for my wife Helena. Please take it, it is yours.'

'Daddy's made necklaces, ear-rings, pendants, all sorts of things.' Rosie chipped in.

'Thank you. I know my wife will treasure it – as will I. Now listen, we have to get you and Rosie out of the hospital as quietly as possible. So I thought....'

Later that day, Rosie's father, dressed as a hospital orderly, pushed a wheelchair with a rather ancient-looking patient wrapped in several blankets, out through the main hospital entrance and into a waiting taxi. The Professor, who was looking down from his office window, was relieved when he saw the cab pull away from the curb and leave the hospital grounds.

He was holding the bracelet Rosie's father had made. He looked at it, still amazed at its delicacy, and something compelled him to polish it by rubbing his fingers over the smooth metal. And, while he did so, another very vague, very interesting possibility began to crystallise in his mind. But then his bleep went off and he realised he should have been in surgery ten minutes ago.

*

Saturday morning arrived and so did Sam's friend Alex. He said the drive would probably take about two to two and a half hours depending on the traffic. As was now required for women being driven by a man, the two women had to wear their full durkas and jibas and sit in the back so that they were completely separated from the male driver. The police and MGs used cameras to ensure women didn't sit in the front passenger seat of any vehicle. If caught the fines and on-the-spot beatings could be severe. Sam recalled once seeing a woman receiving lashes beside the motorway on the hard shoulder – the man was being fined but it was the woman who received the beating.

They set off early and were soon on the motorway heading south around the city. Alex was a big guy with curly blond hair. He was a musician whom Sam had become friends with as they often practised the guitar together. However, Alex wasn't a talker and so as they picked up speed on the motorway both Susan and Sam fell quiet and looked out at the passing factories, houses and countryside.

Fifteen minutes into the journey Susan, who had been in hover sleep for most of the night, began to doze off and she lay down with her head on Sam's lap. Sam lifted Susan's jiba and gently stroked her neck and ear. Then, in Susan's mind Sam's hazelnut appeared. Susan didn't know why but in her imagination she always saw – and certainly felt beneath her finger – Sam's clitoris as a tiny, firm hazelnut that always needed to be gently coaxed out of its brown shell. How this association had embedded itself in her mind she had no idea – but it was there, in her thoughts, every time they made love. And now, as her passion grew on the back seat of the car, it was no different. Susan moved her hand beneath Sam's durka and, as was often the case these days, Sam was already very wet and so Susan slipped her finger easily into Sam's vagina.

Up on the motorway embankment the first massive billboard swept past the car. The letters in each word must have been the size of a man and the message was blunt:

> **All Terrorists are Homosexuals!**
>
> **All Homosexuals are Terrorists!**

Sam closed her eyes and abandoned herself to Susan's caresses, but Susan wanted more. She buried herself beneath Sam's durka and pressed her tongue down hard onto Sam's hazelnut. Sam almost melted. Using the fingers of her other hand Susan gently pushed the brown hood of skin up off Sam's clitoris and softly kissed it. Then she massaged it with her tongue until her finger – that was still inside Sam's vagina – felt the contractions of Sam's orgasm.

High up beside the motorway another gigantic billboard swept past, this time declaring,

> **They're not so gay at the end of a rope!**

A moment later, after she had relaxed, Sam lay down and burrowed her way beneath Susan's durka. She found the small chord between her legs and slowly slid Susan's pink tampon out and almost immediately she pushed her tongue deep into Susan. This last week, during the heavy part of Susan's period, Sam found the taste of Susan so exciting, so enticing it was sometimes difficult for her to think of anything else. Once, during the lunch break at school, she was sitting in the staff room with the other teachers vaguely listening to the chatter around her, when she closed her eyes and imagined herself between Susan's legs, and just this act of fantasy caused her to quietly orgasm.

Another billboard which stretched across an overhead bridge proclaimed –

Vaccinate Now! Phone GayCure on 0800 888 666

Alex looked in his rear-view mirror and noticed that both Sam and Susan had disappeared. He quickly glanced behind but saw only a mass of black durka material and so assumed his two passengers had fallen asleep. Both women were indeed exhausted. Almost telepathically they had woken up in the middle of the previous night and made love, so now after Susan climaxed again, they were both so tired they slept for the rest of the journey.

'Hey! You two! Wake up I don't know which way to go!' Alex shouted. Susan sat up and straightened her jiba.

'Where are we?' she yawned.

'We came off the motorway about ten minutes ago but I don't know where to go on these country roads.'

'Just head towards Dimchester.'

'That's what I thought, but what's this village called where your aunt lives?' Alex asked over his shoulder as the car went a little too fast around a bend.

'It's called Maidensbridge,' Susan replied, 'But you've got to turn right before Dimchester – so the map says.'

'OK, Maidensbridge it is.'

Now that they had left the motorway and its cameras, Susan pulled Sam's jiba off and gently lifted her sleeping head onto her lap. Susan ran her fingers through Sam's think, black hair, then lent forward and kissed her cheek. In a soft voice, she said,

'Come on sleepyhead, we're almost there.' Then putting her lips very close to Sam's ear she whispered, 'I love you.' Although her eyes were still closed, Sam smiled.

*

The barge was amazing. If ever a barge could be described as 'cute and cosy', the Professor's was it. It was cute on the outside and cosy on the inside. There were three cosy bedrooms, a cosy lounge, a cosy kitchen, a cosy toilet and shower – everything about it was neat and snug beyond belief. There were even bookshelves loaded with interesting books from astronomy to diseases of the feet. Professor Marshal said that, although she was out of hospital, Rosie still had to remain in bed and do nothing for another two weeks at least, and since he lived only a couple of miles down the canal tow-path, he promised he would call around every couple of days to make sure all was well.

However the very next morning, before he drove to work, the Professor returned with a small satellite dish and a laptop for Rosie. He said that reading books was fine but it was high time Rosie learnt how to use modern technology. Rosie, of course, had heard of computers and seen them but had never used one, so the Professor gave her a few lessons to get her going. But as is often the case with young people and computers it doesn't take long before they are teaching you, and Rosie was soon showing the Professor how to improve the image quality and speed of the processor.

Very satisfied that his idea of giving Rosie a laptop had worked so well, the Professor left for St. Mary's. Rosie and her father settled in to their new home and almost immediately Mr. Harrison set to work making his unique jewellery. After a couple of days he set up a small table on the canal tow-path where he tried selling his work. A few people out walking their dogs stopped and marvelled at his handiwork and after three days he had sold two bracelets and a pair of ear-rings.

The fourth day was a Friday and the Professor arrived in the early part of the afternoon. Rosie's father had made a bed up on the sofa for Rosie who sat, as usual, surrounded by books. When Professor Marshal came down into the cosy cabin Rosie was reading. He'd expected her to be using her laptop like all youngsters seemed to do.

'Rosie! Mr. Harrison! How are you both? Sorry I haven't been sooner but there have been far too many emergencies these last few days and I've been getting home rather tired. But Hey! It's Friday afternoon! I thought we could all go for a chug up the canal? What do you say?!'

'Yes!' shouted Rosie enthusiastically.

'O! Before I forget – my wife loved the bracelet and sends her thanks. Now before we start her up and cast off, let's have a cup of tea, I'm parched,' the Professor suggested. Rosie's father put on the kettle and the Professor cheekily asked Rosie,

'So, what have you discovered about how to merge two female haploid cells?'

'That's not what I want to talk about,' Rosie replied with a little smile.

'Oh?' Professor Marshal remarked with some surprise.

'No. You've been rather naughty Professor,' Rosie began a little like a school teacher.

'Oh dear! What have I done now!?'

'Well, today you've said the 'F' word six times.'

'Never!' cried the Professor with mock embarrassment.

'Yes, and I've got it all written down,' Rosie went on as she unfolded a piece of paper and started to read, 'First, this morning when you squeezed toothpaste onto your toothbrush, it fell off and you said 'Oh F-'. Then as you were leaving for work you stopped and picked your nose in the mirror in the hallway, and you made your nose bleed and you shouted 'O F-ing Hell!'

'Rosie!' the Professor cried his eyes almost popping out of his face with astonishment. But Rosie hadn't finished,

'Then, as you were driving to work you passed a police car and under your breath you told the policeman to 'F-off'. That was number three. The fourth time you said it was when a man stepped off the pavement and you shouted that he should 'Open his F-ing eyes!' The fifth time was when a Blue priest said he wanted to purify you as you walked into the hospital – you were not very polite to him, you said he should go and –'

'Yes! Yes! I know what I said to him. But Rosie! How!?'

'Then the phone rang in your office and you said Mrs. Bailey's blood pressure was 'too F-ing high to operate', and you would only open her up after she'd been given 10 milligrams of amlodipine − which, I think was the correct decision. So you see, you've been extremely naughty.'

'But Rosie! How on Earth do you know all this! It's crazy! It's not possible!' the Professor exclaimed bewildered.

'Oh but it is! Watch!' Rosie said with excitement as she leant forward and opened up the laptop. The Professor came and sat next to Rosie to see how all this craziness was possible.

'You see I found this site and I got a month's free trial,' explained Rosie.

'A free trial of what?' the Professor asked still totally puzzled.

'A buzzbot!' Rosie replied.

'A what!?'

'They call it a nanoscopic video camera. It sits in a buzzbot − it's a flying robot really, but it's smaller and quieter that a housefly − and the most awesome thing is you can control where it flies from your laptop! Watch! Look, this is the buzzbot I followed you to work with this morning. I left it by the window in your office to charge up − it uses light energy, it should be fully charged by now.'

Up on the full screen of Rosie's laptop came a crystal clear image of the Professor's office.

'Oh my god! It's my office!'

'Watch this Professor − let's take off!' The image on the laptop then wobbled a bit and started showing various views of the Professor's office which could only have been taken by something flying around near the ceiling.

'I don't believe this!' Professor Marshal said with astonishment, his eyes fixed to the screen. However, the image suddenly showed a flash of blueness.

'What was that? In the corner?' the Professor exclaimed. Rosie pressed a few keys on the laptop and the buzzbot turned and showed a Blue Priest opening and closing the drawers in Professor Marshal's desk.

'Hey! Get out of my office!' the enraged Professor shouted at the laptop, 'Stop rooting through my things! The dam cheek!'

'Do you want the microphone on?' Rosie asked and without waiting for an answer she tapped a few keys and whispered to the Professor that he should say something.

'Hey you! Get the fuck out of my office!' yelled the Professor. The Blue Priest instantly stopped, looked around and above him and, seeing nothing, he fled from the room shouting 'Ah! The Devs!'

Rosie looked at the Professor and said cheekily,

'That's now seven times.'

The Professor smiled but didn't reply.

*

Maidensbridge was indeed a small, isolated place but, surprisingly, it was quite pretty. There were lots of tall, ancient trees that lined the narrow roads to the farms. The farms themselves were widely scattered between small hills and the surrounding land hadn't been cleared of all its tress; indeed many of the farms still had their own orchards, so the whole place almost had the feeling of being in a very thin forest. At the very centre of the village the road just came to a dead end right outside the one dilapidated general store. Next door to this was a garage selling diesel and, set back half-way into a field, a mechanic's shed with an assortment of rusting frames of metal that long ago had been vehicles. Susan guided Alex past the store and down a narrow, two-wheeled track to one of the farms. A flood of fond childhood memories swirled around inside Susan's head of all the summers, autumns and springs she had spent here climbing trees, eating fruit, riding old Bonny and hiding in the straw in the barn. However, her most cherished memory was of her auntie, because, even when she'd been naughty, her auntie had always forgiven her with a kiss, a hug and a smile.

Susan spotted Auntie Jane chopping wood beside the large farmhouse. It was a lovely old house, half brick and half wood, with a mossy, tiled roof that sagged with age. Susan impulsively lent forward over Alex's shoulder and pressed the horn on the steering wheel. Auntie Jane looked up and waved. Susan pressed the horn some more out of sheer fun and delight at seeing her Auntie after so long. When the car stopped she leapt out, threw her jiba in the air and ran and hugged and kissed her Auntie Jane. Her auntie looked like a typical farmer – rubber boots, thick trousers, a jumper full of holes and wild, white hair. Sam got out and she too pulled off her jiba and almost ripped her durka off and threw it into the boot of Alex's car. Susan then brought Sam and Alex over to meet her Auntie Jane.

'Don't worry lass, you don't have to wear that stupid thing here,' Auntie Jane said to Sam as they kissed each other on the cheek.

'Thank god for that!' Sam replied, 'I don't know why, but it always makes me feel I'm being preparing for the grave.'

'Aye, I know what you mean lass. On my land you can swing naked from tree-to-tree for all I care!' Auntie Jane laughed, 'Only when you go to the shop, will you have to dress like the phantom o' the opera.'

'Auntie?' Susan asked as she sniffed the air, 'What's that funny smell?'

'Ah dinna worry about that – now and again when the wind's blowin' in a certain direction we get a whiff of one of the city's rubbish tips – but it never lasts. You get used to it. Now let's go on in and have a cup of tea shall we?'

After all the introductions were over they went inside. Susan however ran ahead shouting over her shoulder 'Where's the baby!?' Auntie Jane called out she wasn't to make so much noise because the baby had only just fallen asleep.

Inside the large heated kitchen, in the corner, Auntie Jane had set up a cot on an old sofa. Susan was first at the cot, her eyes wide with anticipation – and the sleeping baby did not disappoint.

'O look Sam! She's so sweet! O Sam she's beautiful! So perfect!'

'She's gorgeous!' Sam said peering down over Susan's shoulder.

'Look at her tiny fingers!' Susan marvelled.

'How old is she?' Alex asked.

'She's almost 6 weeks.'

'Have you given her a name?' Susan asked unable to take her eyes from the baby.

'That's what I hoped we could all do this week end – find the wee mite a name?' Auntie Jane suggested.

'I want to hold her! Can I?' Susan pleaded. But Auntie Jane wouldn't hear of it – these moments of peace were rare and she needed a break.

When, an hour later, the baby did wake, Susan was immediately there and she lifted it gently out of the cot. The baby curled its small hand around Susan's finger and smiled – and the bond was cemented. Susan became almost ecstatic with love for this so, so innocent and unblemished creature. From the moment it awoke in the early afternoon to the early evening, Susan carried the baby everywhere. Occasionally Sam was given a turn but it wasn't long before the child was back in Susan's arms. She almost seemed to glow motherhood.

That evening after supper Auntie Jane prepared the baby's bottle and Susan fed it until the 'wee mite' fell asleep. With the baby asleep in Susan's arms the adults quietly discussed their suggestions for a name. After about five or so names were put forward and rejected, someone asked about the baby's real mother.

'Well, that's a muckle of a mystery if ever there was,' Auntie Jane sighed, 'The poor woman was in rags. She had a affie cut across her head, but she had nowt on her to say who she was or where she was from. The only thing she had, besides the bairn in her belly, was this...'

Auntie Jane stood up and brought something from the mantelpiece and handed it to Sam.

'It's beautiful,' Sam said genuinely impressed, 'It's some sort of bracelet.'

'Aye y'right – she was wearing it round her wrist. I thought I'd better take it as an heirloom for the baby because one day she's sure ta ask where she came from.'

'But Auntie – you know I'd like to steal the baby from you,' Susan began with a cheeky smile, 'But how will you cope with running the farm and looking after a tiny baby?'

'Susan, I'm a woman – this is what we do. It's true my back's not helping, but I'll manage – if only for the bairn's sake.'

But the bairn still didn't have a name. A few more suggestions later and Susan said, 'How about 'Ellie'?' No one seemed to object so Auntie Jane said she would try it out for a day or two and if it still felt right then Ellie it would be.

The next day, Sunday, Susan insisted on doing everything for the baby – feeding, changing, cuddling, carrying, playing and Sam looked on awestruck at the change that had come over Susan. Sam had never seen her so totally happy. That night in bed Susan wrapped her arms around Sam and whispered, 'I want one!' but Sam was thinking about what might happen in the morning when they were due to leave. And sure enough when she woke on the Monday morning, Susan was very subdued. She still, of course, went first thing as she had done every morning into her aunt's bedroom to check on 'Ellie', but she didn't bubble with her usual selfless enthusiasm. And when the time came for her and Sam to leave, Susan threw her arms around Auntie Jane and broke into the most heart-rendering sobs as though she was being forced to abandon her own child. Sam tried comforting her but that only made it worse. On the journey back to the city Susan just lay with her head on Sam's lap, saying nothing, struggling to control her anguish and tears, and for most of the time she wasn't successful.

*

'Rosie, you know those fuzzbot things? Would you show a rather slow learner like me how to order one and how they work?' Professor Marshal asked on his next visit to the barge.

'You mean buzzbots?'

'Yes, those buzzbots,' replied the Professor.

'Why? Who do you want to spy on?' Rosie asked cheekily.

'Rosie, your mind is too suspicious. But, now you've mentioned it, don't you realise these nano buzzbits could mean the end of privacy, of confidentiality – it could be the beginning of a world where everyone can secretly watch everyone else.'

'But wouldn't that be a good thing Professor – to live in a world without secrets? Where secrets were no longer needed? Where people had to be open and honest about everything?' Rosie asked.

'Maybe, maybe. But before that day comes I want you to show me how to get my very own buzzbite.'

The process, Rosie told him, was really very simple. The Professor had to link his own laptop to a buzzbot using an ID number given to him by the buzzbot manufacturers, pay a small sum of money and wait for it to arrive by post. The Professor duly did as Rosie instructed and two days later he signed a docket pushed under his nose by a courier, who then handed him a small, fat envelope. Now all he needed to do was key in his ID and away it should go. The instructions said so long as there was light falling on it from above, it had the power to fly. He tried it first around his own house and was amazed at the results. He spied on his dog lying in its basket in the kitchen, his wife – still in bed – reading her horoscope in the newspaper. He flew it under doors, through open windows, under tables and chairs and out into the garden, then up to the roof, down a chimney and back out into the living room. It was totally, totally addictive and, even though the buzzbot had the top speed of a bluebottle, he could still see everything in sharp, clear focus and after a couple of hours the Professor was ready for some serious spying.

He first found the exact coordinates of Dr. Abdulla-Smith's surgery in Farley Street, keyed them in to his buzzbot and pressed enter. The buzzbot, which was in his garden, immediately shot upwards and the Professor watched on his laptop as his garden became one of scores and then hundreds in a patchwork of green lawns. The Professor sat in his study at home watching everything, still astounded that so small a thing could see every detail of its surroundings and be so easy to control.

After roughly twenty minutes the buzzbot was hovering over the good Doctor's Farley St., surgery. The Professor now had to find a way in. The roof, he argued, wouldn't be a good place to look because it was meant to keep out the heavy rain so everything would be sealed. So he sent the buzzbot down at the rear of the building and, sure enough, on the first floor there was a window ajar. The Professor guided the buzzbot through the gap and saw he was in some sort of office. The Professor was interested in the basement because that was where he hoped Dr. Abdulla-Smith stored his cadavers, so he flew the buzzbot down to the bottom of the closed office door where, fortunately, he found plenty of space to fly under and out. Now on the Professor's laptop screen were some stairs and it didn't take the Professor long to whizz the buzzbot down the stairwell to the basement. However, this door was a much tighter fit and there was no room underneath, but above the door was a small air vent with enough space for the buzzbot to fly through. The Professor found himself looking at a large room with six massive drawers all along one wall. He knew immediately he was in the right place because it looked very like the morgue in St. Mary's. He flew the buzzbot up and sideways and what now appeared on his laptop screen made the blood drain from his face and a feeling of grotesque sickness to gnaw through his heart. He pressed the Record option on his laptop screen. He moved the buzzbot closer as though being nearer to what was going on would make it less disgusting, but the opposite was the case. Despite the utterly heinous scene he was witnessing, the Professor kept on recording. When he was sure he had captured enough on video the Professor moved the buzzbot back through the air-vent and out of Dr. Abdulla-Smith's surgery up into the blue, free sky where the mania of human depravity could not reach. He had got what he wanted – and on his very first visit. Of course, he hadn't, in his wildest dreams, expected to find the answers to his suspicions so quickly and so easily. But now that he knew what was happening, he had to decide what to do with this information, because, if used correctly, it could, and it should, open people's eyes to the truth, but if used with ignorance it would, and it could backfire and cause a uncontrollable wave of confusion and suffering. So what was he to do now? And there was another problem – how could he verify what he had recorded?

*

Susan and Sam had been back in the city for almost a week. Sam had returned to work and Susan had stayed indoors – it was just too risky for her to be out on the street. Since the 'incident' in Strafalgar Square, the authorities had doubled the number of MGs on patrol. On almost every corner they were randomly stopping women, checking their IDs and ensuring they were wearing the correct 'insignia of honour'.

In between thinking of little 'Ellie' and writing a letter to her Auntie Jane, Susan prepared supper, but Sam did not return home at the usual time. Susan thought she remembered Sam saying something about a staff meeting after school, but she wasn't sure. She rang Sam's mobile but there was no reply – which was to be expected if she was in a meeting. An hour later Sam had still not returned and

Susan felt a small flutter of fear. She tried Sam's mobile again, but again there was no answer. Maybe, Susan argued, she'd gone with some of the other teachers for a coffee after the meeting – but, if so, why hadn't she called to tell Susan she'd be late? Susan stopped trying to keep their supper warm and after yet another hour she began to get really worried. She called Alex, who fortunately, lived only a few streets away. He said there was probably a very ordinary reason why Sam was late and Susan shouldn't get too anxious. Not really reassured Susan waited. Twenty minutes later she called Alex back and said there was still no sign of Sam and that they must do something because it was very unlike Sam to behave in this way.

It was now getting late, curfew was in two hours and although Susan called several of Sam's friends no one knew where she was or where she could be. Susan called Alex again and this time she sounded so distraught Alex agreed to come over and be with her until Sam came home. Fifteen minutes later Alex arrived and gave Susan a comforting hug telling her Sam was probably in some secret night spot dancing and enjoying herself. But the truth was he too was getting concerned. Sam's flat was on the first floor and the living room overlooked most of the street. Outside it was beginning to get dark and Susan kept going to the window to scan the street for any signs of her friend. Another hour went by and still no Sam.

Maybe they should call the police? Susan suggested, but Alex said that, given the present circumstances, was probably the worst thing they could do – if they discovered Susan in Sam's flat they would both never see the light of day again. Susan showed Alex some photos of 'Ellie' that her Auntie Jane had sent, and for a short while they forgot about Sam. Then Susan looked at the clock – it was ten minutes to curfew and outside it was already night. The six or so street lamps all came on simultaneously. Susan checked the street again. Nothing.

However, just as she was about to leave the window she noticed a car violently swerve into their street. It screeched to a halt some distance from the flat. One of the car doors opened accompanied by ugly, aggressive shouting and something large and lifeless was thrown out onto the pavement. A man got out and viciously kicked whatever or whoever was on the ground, shouting,

'You fucking black whore! Next time keep your mouth shut! Black bitch!'

He climbed back into the car and slammed the door shut. The car's tyres squealed as it accelerated and shot past the flat and disappeared.

Susan leapt down the stairs and out into the street and she ran yelling and screaming towards the dark heap on the pavement. She got there and uncovered Sam's bleeding face.

'NO! NO! NO!' Susan screamed as though her very heart was on fire with despair.

Alex arrived and felt for Sam's pulse.

'Shit! Those fucking bastards! Susan! There's...there's a faint pulse! But I'm not sure! Quick we've got to get her to hospital! I'll get my car!'

Alex ran to his car and was soon parked alongside the pavement. Carefully they lifted the unconscious Sam onto the back seat and drove to the nearest Accident & Emergency. Susan was crying with an anguish so deep it had robbed her of all expression. She sat in the back like someone possessed, rocking backwards and forwards, stroking Sam's wounded head, saying over and over 'No!...No!... No!'

'Susan!' Alex shouted. But she was too upset to even hear him. However Alex knew it was imperative he got through to her to make her listen, so he bellowed, 'SUSAN!'

She turned to look at him.

'Listen Susan! We've got to be careful at the hospital!' Alex shouted over his shoulder as he drove, 'They'll want to know how it happened. We can't tell them the truth because they'd never believe us and if they did they'd only bring in the police to investigate. The police would recognise you and all hell would break loose. We have to tell the same story. We have to be consistent. We'll say we were walking home just before curfew along the main road where you live and she was hit by a car which sped off. A hit-and-run case – I'm sure they get loads of them. So remember Susan, say nothing but if they do ask you, you have to say it was a hit and run accident OK!? We didn't get the number of the car because it all happened so fast! Do you understand?' Susan slowly nodded.

An hour later a grim looking doctor emerged from the examination room where they had taken Sam.

'Are you related to the patient?' the doctor asked Alex and Susan.

'No, we're just good friends.' Alex replied.

'How is she?' Susan asked anxiously.

'She'll live – but only just. Broken arm, three snapped ribs, multiple bruising, dislocated wrist, but fortunately, only minor internal injuries. She's lucky. But you are?' the doctor asked Alex.

'Alex.'

'Well Alex, I have to be honest with you – I've seen many hit-and-run cases in my time, but her injuries seem wholly inconsistent with this type of accident. They're more consistent with someone being beaten.

The majority of the injuries are to the upper torso, whereas when a pedestrian is hit by a car, most of the severe injuries occur below the waist. You are sure this is a hit-and-run incident?'

'Yes...yes , it must have been the way she fell I guess.' Alex lied.

'Hummm...and another thing that seems strange is that you said you were walking when the car struck?'

'Yes,' Alex replied trying to sound truthful.

'With a woman? After curfew? – that doesn't seem right?'

'The bus we'd been on got stuck in traffic, so it was already late when we got off and we were hurrying home before curfew started.'

'I see...So you got off the bus and were walking home?' the doctor asked again.

'That's right, along the main road.' Alex replied.

'Then why is this young lady,' here the doctor pointed at Susan, 'not wearing her jiba? She could not have been walking the streets uncovered, you know that.'

'I used it to make a bandage,' Susan quickly lied, 'But it must have fallen off as we were lifting Sam into Alex's car.'

'Hummm I see. Well, all I can say is that she's lucky to have had you two friends close by,' said the doctor finally smiling.

'I'm not leaving the hospital. I'm not leaving Sam. I want to be here when she wakes up.' Susan announced as though there was going to be no discussion.

'Well, young lady...if you are to stay, you will have to wear some face covering. I think one of the nurses might lend you a spare jiba from the laundry room – I'll see what I can do.'

'Please, can I see her?' Susan pleaded.

'Not at the moment I'm afraid, the nurses are still busy putting on the arm cast and dressing her wounds – don't forget she's still unconscious. Let's see what she's like in an hour – I'll try and have a word with one of the nurses.'

Alex and Susan went to look for a hospital kiosk to get some coffee.

'Susan,' Alex said in a low voice, 'You have to get that jiba the doctor talked about – you can't risk anyone recognising you.'

'I will, I will, don't worry.'

'And,' Alex continued now in a whisper, 'one of us has to be here when she wakes up – in case Sam tells them a different story – if she does then we'll all be blown out of the water.'

'Don't worry Alex, I'll stay. As soon as she's awake I'll tell her. I'm not leaving here without her – even if I have to sleep on the floor for a month. I'm not letting Sam out of my sight.'

'You must love her an awful lot?' Alex remarked.

'Isn't loving someone the only thing that gives life any sense?'

'I suppose.'

'And yes, I do love her – if it was possible I would have her children.'

'You're lucky you found each other,' Alex responded.

'I know, and I don't intend to lose her to racist thugs,' Susan answered with suppressed rage.

Susan spent three days and nights on a stretcher bed in the same room as Sam. On the morning of the fourth day Sam opened her eyes and seeing Susan lying in a bed near the floor, dozing, Sam croaked

'Hello'. Susan's eyes instantly sprang open and she threw off a blanket and ran to Sam's bed and kissed her. The doctors were pleased that Sam had regained consciousness but they said it would still be four to six weeks before they could even consider letting her go home. And even after she went home, they said, she couldn't return to work for at least three or four months – it all depended on whether there were any complications in her recovery. And the one complication no one expected was Sam couldn't walk.

*

How could he verify what he had recorded? How to answer this question gave the Professor many sleepless nights during the week that followed. Why? Because he knew people could easily turn around and say that the whole thing had been fabricated, rehearsed and staged by some sad, unemployed actors paid for by the Professor. It was a vexing problem. After what he had seen with the Blue Priests searching his office in the hospital when he was absent, and what he had now recorded, he kept his laptop at home under lock and key. He knew his laptop contained dynamite, but the Professor didn't know how or when to explode it.

On Saturday morning he cycled from his house, along the canal towpath, to visit Rosie and her father. Rosie was looking much better and the dressing on her head was now quite small and her dark hair around the incision was beginning to grow back nicely. Rosie's father now had quite a collection of his special 'electric' jewellery – as Rosie called it. The table he had set up on the towpath was now full of various bracelets, necklaces and ear-rings, each one beautiful and, more importantly, unique. The Professor was keenly aware that Rosie's father didn't have a real income – in fact, he had never in his life had a real income, since Untouchables were barred from entering any of the professions – even barred from attending school. As Roja they were expected to do that for which, other castes believed, they were born – cleaning the streets, collecting the city's refuse, unblocking sewers, digging graves, in other words, doing all the dirty work the 'higher' castes didn't want to do.

The Professor found Rosie's father down in the cabin cleaning the small port-hole windows.

'Mr. Harrison,' the Professor began with a pretend serious smile.

'Professor?'

'Could you please stand up and put out your arms like this,' the Professor asked holding out his arms in front of him like someone about to dive into water.

'Are you going to tickle daddy?' Rosie scolded.

'No, of course not Rosie,' the Professor replied smiling. He then said to Rosie's father,

'Now Mr. Harrison, I want you to keep your hands as still as you possibly can.'

'What's this for Professor?' Rosie's father asked.

'I'm not sure – maybe nothing – we'll see. Now keep them as still as possible.... Hummm...very good, excellent. Good, you can put them down.'

The professor then went to the table and took out of his pocket a small, jumbled handful of paper clips. He placed them in a mound on the table then he sprinkled a tiny amount of sugar over the heap of paperclips. The white sugar crystals bounced down between the clips and came to rest on the table.

'There, Mr. Harrison. Now what I'd like you to do is to take these surgical tweezers,' here the Professor took from his inside pocket a long, thin black leather case. He opened it and slid out a pair of very delicate, fine tweezers and handed them to Rosie's father.

'What I'd like you to do is use the tweezers to pick up ten grains of sugar, without touching or moving a single paperclip.' the Professor instructed.

'But why? What for Professor?' Rosie's father asked bewildered.

'Don't worry - I just need to see something.'

'Ten sugar grains?'

'Yes. But you mustn't move a single paperclip remember,' the Professor reminded him.

Rosie's father leant forward with the tweezers and, without any difficulty, he delicately extracted ten sugar grains from the tangle of paperclips. Not a single clip was touched or moved.

'Excellent. That was with your right hand. Can you now do the same thing but holding the tweezers with your left hand?'

Without hesitating Rosie's father held the tweezers in his left hand and, just as before, he delicately picked out from the criss-cross jumble of clips, ten sugar grains without touching or moving a single paperclip.

'Excellent Mr. Harrison, very good indeed,' the Professor said as he sat down opposite Rosie's father and he continued, 'You see, from the extremely delicate work you put into your jewellery, I could tell you were probably ambidextrous.'

'What does that mean?' asked Rosie's father.

'It means you've got two right hands dad!' Rosie chipped in.

'Yes, that's it. It means you can use either hand to perform extremely precise movements. Now here's my idea. As you can probably guess when operating on a person's brain you need to have infinite patience and, most importantly, a very steady hand. For over a month now I have been without an assistant in surgery – there just aren't any coming through from the medical schools at the moment, neurosurgery scares them off I guess. So I was wondering if you would like to be my assistant – or at least try it for a while. I could train you up – I promise it's not too difficult and you would receive a regular salary. I do about three to four operations a week but the hours can be erratic – sometimes ten hours at a stretch, but it's fascinating work. So, what do you say?'

Rosie's father was, of course, more than willing to give it a try but there was, he said, one problem – he couldn't leave Rosie alone on the barge while he worked at the hospital.

'Of course not,' the Professor replied, 'on those days we operate, just bring Rosie with you – I'm sure Rosie wouldn't mind if I gave her my hospital library card, would you Rosie?' the professor asked.

'No way! All day in the medical library! Heaven!' Rosie exclaimed ecstatically.

So it was agreed. On Monday the Professor would show Rosie's father the operating theatre and go through the names of some of the instruments he would be using and how to use them. If all went well he could be assisting in his first operation by the end of the week. Rosie couldn't wait.

*

'This is the lounge, and through here, is the kitchen. There's an airing cupboard under the stairs that comes in very handy...'

Susan was showing some prospective tenants around the flat. She and Sam were moving out and going to live with Susan's Auntie Jane. It had been three months since the attack on Sam and she was still in a wheelchair. Some of the doctors said she would never walk again, some others said it was just a matter of time before she was back on her feet – but the truth was no one knew. Her broken arm was now out of its cast but it was still painful especially if she moved it the wrong way in bed. However, her spirit had definitely been badly shaken and Susan would sometimes find her sitting quietly, tears running down her cheeks – something Sam had never done before. Sam had given up her part time teaching job so they were going to need some income, however small, and the rent from the flat would help.

Although Auntie Jane was horrified at what had happened to Sam, she wrote back saying she was thrilled they were coming ('and', she'd written in brackets, 'Ellie was thrilled too!') and they could stay for as long as they wanted and if that meant forever then she would be doubly thrilled.

A week later they hired a van and Alex (together with some other friends who'd come to help and say goodbye) loaded a small collection of boxes containing mostly clothes and books into the back of the van. Last in was Sam's wheel chair. Then Alex carried Sam and sat her in the front seat in the middle between Susan and himself. After a lot of hugs and kisses from friends, they waved goodbye and left.

For both Sam and Susan it was like they were emigrating. Although the journey was just over a couple of hours in the same country, it felt like they were moving out of a perpetual shadow into sunshine. It was, they hoped, to be a transition from something crushing the spirit to something elevating, or freeing it. Over the years the city had imperceptibly become a place of suffocating madness and oppression – especially for women. A feeling of apathetic acceptance of how things were, seemed to grind its way into everyone's lives, so much so, they came to perceive what was happening to them as ordained by a divine power. Somehow people had forgotten they could have some control over their lives, some say in the way their society grew and developed. Democracy had petered out through lack of interest. Online elections had become just one more way – among billions of ways – the masses could entertain themselves. Analysing different political arguments and positions and judging the merits or disadvantages of each, was a skill of the distant, nebulous past. And anyway such a skill, if it ever did re-emerge, would be seen as useless, obsolete and, quite frankly, boring. People's attention span now lasted only as long as it took to tap a screen and move on to something more bizarre, more grotesque or even more revolting. As Susan's boss had once yelled, people wanted to watch things that would make them vomit and shit their pants all at the same time – that's what brought success in this world, that's what made the dollars flow.

As they sped south down the motorway both Susan and Sam, and to some extent Alex – who, of course, was driving – were lost in their own thoughts and emotions. But, however disparate they were as individuals, they all unconsciously shared a feeling of profound change – that, as they silently watched the kilometres before them vanish beneath the wheels, their lives had now taken a direction towards a different definition of sanity.

*

'Spiritual antibiotics! What a load of superstitious crap! Pseudo-science at its worst!' the Professor said to himself as he watched, spellbound, for the sixth time a recording on his laptop. He had been 'buzzboting' again. A week after he had recorded the scene of depravity in Dr. Abdulla-Smith's private morgue, the Professor had decided to fly the buzzbot into the good Doctor's office, to see if the Doctor himself was aware of what was going on three floors below him in the basement. However, the good Doctor must have been away on business because the Professor had to leave the buzzbot lying dormant on an upper windowsill for several days before there was any activity worth recording. Then on about the fourth day the buzzbot sent a signal to the Professor's laptop that there was something happening in its vicinity and did he want the buzzbot to record it? The professor had used a default setting which allowed his laptop to automatically respond with a 'Yes' should it receive such a request. The Professor was, of course, in surgery (it was also Rosie's father's second day as the Professor's assistant) when the signal from the buzzbot came through, so it was only when the Professor returned home did he find the recording waiting for him.

The buzzbot had hovered, as instructed, near the ceiling of the office and it had filmed and recorded a conversation between Dr. Abdulla-Smith and Jones -

'Anyway this is not a time for doubts Jones – this contract could secure the firm's fortunes – and yours – for decades to come.'

'I understand that Sir. It's just that if we are careless it may go against us in the future.'

'Well, we're not going to be careless now are we? – that's your job. Look, there are customers out there – patients – who will die if they don't receive a donated organ.'

'But what if that donated organ, which came from us, ended up killing thousands?'

'What if! What if!' There are thousands of 'What ifs?' in life! But no one will ever know which 'what if' was our fault – will they?'

'I think they could Sir.'

'What, trace the source back to us?'

'Most definitely. Any MRSA infected organs we send to clients could one day be traced back to this surgery.'

'Now there I have to disagree with you Jones. You see these cadavers that come to us from the hospitals, have died because there were no medical antibiotics to destroy the MRSA bacteria. But when we receive them downstairs I always allow Blue Priests – and sometimes even the Grand Muftin himself – to come and purify the body. Each corpse undergoes a purification ceremony with spiritual antibiotics that clean the bodies of infection and, at the same time, of evil.'

'That may be possible Sir, but one day these spiritual antibiotics may not work.'

'Yes Jones that's possible, 'one day',' the good Doctor replied with a hint of irritation in his voice, and he continued, 'but that's already been taken care of. If 'one day' we get an enquiry from some overseas government or some such, we can always blame the bad management, or the poor record-keeping, or the lame computer skills of clerical staff in the hospitals we do business with. For all the investigators would ever know we accepted the cadavers in good faith believing them to be free of infection.'

'Hummm...'

'You seem doubtful Jones?'

'But it would not be too difficult for an investigator to see a pattern in the infection.'

'What do you mean? What 'pattern'?'

'Well, I've noticed that all those organs which we definitely know to be infected with MRSA – are somehow sent to those countries overseas, that have rejected, indeed have outlawed, Blue Dog Chaothicism. We could be accused of deliberately spreading disease to countries we have declared as Blasphemous States.'

'Are you saying Jones there is some global conspiracy theory going on here and that its epicentre is right here in this room?'

'It is feasible Sir.'

The good Doctor opened a drawer in his desk and took out a small revolver. He pointed it at Jones and said,

'You're right Jones, it is feasible. But at least your organs won't be infected,' and he fired a single shot that killed Jones outright. Doctor Abdulla-Smith quietly replaced the revolver into the drawer and closed it. Then he leant forward and clicked a button on the intercom.

'Baker?'

'Sir?' came a mechanical reply.

'Are there any spare drawers in the morgue?'

At this point the buzzbot sent a signal that its power was running low and it needed to find a source of light. Automatically it headed back towards the windowsill where it landed and entered sleep-charge mode. It was here the Professor had found it when he came home and turned on his laptop. It took the Professor a mere twenty minutes to fly his new toy – the buzzbot – back to his kitchen table at home.

He had recorded a genuine murder. The murderer and the victim were easily identifiable. Should he inform the police? But what if....? What if....?

*

It was early in the morning, not long after breakfast, and Susan was in the vegetable garden behind the farmhouse with her Auntie Jane. They were turning over a fallow area to plant more potatoes. The work was hard but Susan was clearly enjoying the idea of being self-sufficient. She and Sam had already been a couple of weeks on the small-holding and each day Susan was learning the 'art' of cultivation – how and when to store seeds, how and when to plant seeds, how to pollinate, how to watch out for pests, what to plant to naturally ward off parasites or prevent mould, what compost was best for what type of soil – it was indeed, Susan was realising, both an art and a science all in one.

On this particular morning, because the air outside was still a little chilly, Sam had remained inside with Ellie, near the open fire to keep warm. Sam sat in her wheelchair reading while Ellie lay asleep on a thick lambskin rug some distance from the log fire. Susan had been careful to place the fire guard in front of the fire before she left, and anyway, she knew Sam was going to keep a close eye on the baby – a job she had been doing every day over the past two weeks while Susan and her Auntie were away in the fields.

Sam sat and lowered her book to look at Ellie. It was true she was the sweetest thing you could imagine, lots of blonde curls and deep black eyes – even her temperament, when she was awake, seemed to shine through as being a thoughtful, quiet child. She hardly ever cried – just little whimpers now and again that seemed to tear bits off everyone's heart. Sam raised her book and continued reading.

A minute later there was a sudden, loud bang and hiss from the fire and a large glowing ember shot upwards over the top of the fire guard and landed just an inch from Ellie. The sudden noise woke Ellie who began to stir. Instantly the ember started charring down into the lambskin rug and without thinking Sam instinctively leapt up, grabbed Ellie and pulled her out of harm's way into the now empty wheelchair. Sam then flicked the lambskin rug over and knocked the smouldering ember out onto the hearth. She then realised what she was doing – she was standing upright! And she had taken two steps! But, more importantly, she felt no pain, nothing unusual. Could she take another step? Steadying herself on various bits of furniture Sam slowly shuffled her way to the outside door. Behind her Ellie gave a small gurgling sound and when Sam looked round Ellie was wide awake, smiling and kicking her legs in Sam's wheelchair.

An hour later Susan and her Auntie were returning to the farmhouse for a cup of tea. They were talking about the dangers of frost. Susan suddenly stopped and stared at the farmhouse – there in the open doorway stood Sam holding Ellie in her arms!

*

The phone rang in Professor Marshal's office. He wasn't there. His old answer machine began to play its recorded message –

'I'm sorry I'm probably removing someone's brain tumour at the moment, please call back later or leave a short message after the bleep...'

'Hello Professor Marshal, my name's George Martin producer of the programme Action Debates on DDC television. Would you be interested in a live televised debate between yourself and the Grand

Muftin in about a week's time? The theme of the debate would be along the lines 'Is science God's gift or God's curse?' But the precise title would be negotiable. My cell number is 0134 223 4765. Thank you for your time. I look forward to hearing from you.'

It was only later in the day, after a ten hour operation on a young woman to remove a malignant tumour, that Professor Marshal played back the recorded message. He was too tired to speak to anyone and, since he saw he had no appointments in the morning, he decided to call Mr. Martin tomorrow. He went home.

'Valery!' the Professor called to his wife as he closed the front door behind him.

'I'm in the study Henry!'

'Guess what?'

'You've banged the car again?' his wife shouted.

'No,' the Professor said as he entered the library, 'No, they want me on the box again, next week.'

'Don't tell me,' his wife smiled, 'now they want you to enter a neuroscientists-have-got-talent competition?'

'Better than that – they want me on Action Debate to debate about science with the Grand Muftin.'

'The Grand Muftin?' his wife asked surprised.

'Yes, he's the new head of the Blue Dog Church.'

'I know who he is Henry – he's a dangerous fool who still thinks women fly around on broomsticks. You'd better be careful.'

'Oh I don't think there's anything to worry about Valery – it could be fun.'

'Hummm... he probably thinks it's fun to burn off women's genitals. I'm telling you Henry these Chaothicist people are dangerous.'

'Maybe...anyway, what's for supper?'

The following morning the Professor arrived early at the hospital and he glanced at his appointments. His morning was free but in the afternoon he was due to operate on a woman who had lost her sight because of a misdiagnosed tumour – if he was careful there was a slim chance he might be able to partially restore the poor woman's sight – it all depended on what he found when he opened her up. He called George Martin.

'Mr. Martin?'

'Professor Marshal! Good of you to call,'

'I hope it's not too early?'

'Not at all. Clearly you got my message. Have you thought it over?'

'Yes, in a manner of speaking, I have.' the Professor replied cautiously.

'I can hear the 'but' in the background.'

'Indeed. What puzzles me is why have you asked me? There are plenty of eminent scientists to choose from, why me?'

'Well we've had plenty of physicists and astronomers and biologists on our screens over the years, but no one's really crossed swords with a neurosurgeon before. Since you made that documentary last year your work has become famous the world over – and now there's your book. I've read most of it and it was while reading that I had the idea that you, being a neurosurgeon, might be able to bring a fresh perspective to the old debate between science and religion. And, in your book, I feel your sub-text very much places medicine as the only viable alternative to superstition.'

'That's nicely put.'

'Can I take that as a 'yes' you'd like to come on the show?'

'Maybe. But first tell me something about my opponent – this new Grand Muftin?'

'Well we know he's been in the church since its inception and he's been the driving force behind much of the gains the Blue Dog Temple has made over the years. There's no doubt its becoming a popular – if aggressive – presence in people's lives. The Menstrual Curfew Ordinances passed recently, were all a direct result of his growing power in government. There have been rumours – unsubstantiated of course – that there is not a single piece of legislation that doesn't pass before his eyes prior to its reaching parliament. He's also said to be an able scholar of science and holds several honourary degrees at a number of prestigious universities.'

'But isn't it unusual for a religious figure to expose themselves to public debate like this – I can't recall a single instance of it happening before?' the Professor queried.

'But that's why this is a unique opportunity for someone like yourself to grill the guy about what he is trying to do – in every other way he's totally unaccountable. And between you and me, he's an odd sort of fish as he seems to actively crave publicity.'

'Look, I can't deny I'm interested, but I'd like a little time to mull it over.'

'Of course. Could you let me know by – say – tomorrow?'

'Yes, tomorrow's fine. I'll call you on this number'

'Great – I look forward to your decision.'

The professor hung up. He drummed his fingers on his desk, swivelled his chair around and stared out the window into the sky. He watched a passenger jet cut in and out of the clouds on its way to Heathbow. On an impulse he turned and switched on his desk computer. He went to the most comprehensive search engine and typed in 'The New Grand Muftin'. Up came a web page with the rather grandiose title –

'The Grand Muftin – Ayatollah Hussein-McDonald III'

And below this was a large photo-portrait of the Grand Muftin himself, smiling into the camera, fully robed in the ostentatious regalia of his new office. The Professor stared at the face and slowly a chill crept down his back – he knew this face from somewhere – then recognition hit him,

'Oh fuck!'

*

Later that same day, after he had operated on the misdiagnosed woman, Professor Marshal went to see Rosie and her father.

'Rosie!? Mr. Harrison!? Anyone at home!?' the Professor called as he stepped onto the barge. There was no reply. Down in the cabin he found everything nice and tidy and Rosie's laptop open on the table. The Professor realised they had probably gone for small walk to get some fresh air and to give Rosie some gentle exercise now she was back on her feet. He decided to wait. He idly nudged the mouse attached to the laptop and was attracted by what appeared on the screen. It was the facsimile text of what looked like a very old book called 'Artificial Parthenogenesis and Fertilisation' by someone called Loeb. 'What was Rosie into now?' the Professor thought to himself and he recalled Rosie's bursting enthusiasm many weeks ago about diploid and haploid cells. So she was only doing what he had suggested and that was researching the topic.

Up on deck he heard footsteps. Rosie was first to clamber down into the main cabin and when she saw the Professor sitting next to her laptop she called out enthusiastically and she ran into the cabin to explain what she'd found.

'Professor! I think it's possible! There's this book that describes loads of experiments where egg cells are fertilised without a male cell going anywhere near a female cell! All we need to do is use these ideas with what they do in IVF and it should work!'

'Rosie! Rosie! Calm down! Remember, I'm a slow thinker! What are you talking about?' the Professor objected.

'Remember – female haploid plus female haploid – a half plus a half gives a whole. Fertilisation has evolved in nature to be male haploid plus female haploid – but that is still a half plus a half gives a whole. They've managed to do IVF outside the womb between a female egg and a male sperm, now we need to show it's possible between a female egg and another female egg! It will work! I know it!'

'Look Rosie, as a junior doctor, before I became a neurosurgeon, I spent some years doing IVF, and it can be quite tricky to get the conditions just right for conception to occur. You'll have to do some more research on what would happen to the sex chromosomes if two female eggs, from different mothers, were to unite. Now Rosie, I need to speak with your dad,' the Professor ruffled Rosie's hair affectionately and turned to her father who was sitting bemused at his super clever daughter.

'Mr. Harrison – Oh I think it's time I called you by your fist name – would that be alright with you?' the Professor asked a little embarrassed.

'Of course,' Rosie's father replied smiling.

'Good. Well, Joshua, the real reason I've dropped by is to ask you if you would have any objection to my wife and I...coming to live on the barge for a while with you and Rosie?'

'Are we going on holiday!?' Rosie asked excitedly.

'Not exactly,' answered the Professor.

'Of course not,' Rosie's father replied and he added, 'If you don't mind me saying Professor, that's a silly question, it's your barge after all.'

'Thank you. It's really just a precautionary measure and it's probably wholly unnecessary.'

'Are you hiding from someone Professor?' Rosie asked.

'I don't know yet – probably not – probably I'm being too paranoid, but I just don't want to take unnecessary risks.'

'If you're in any kind of trouble Professor me and Rosie are always here to help.'

'That's kind of you,' answered the Professor and he coughed and said to Rosie's father, 'Joshua, could we talk up on deck for a minute, what I have to say is only for adult ears – sorry Rosie,' the Professor said glancing at Rosie.

Up outside the two men stepped from the barge and strolled down the tow path talking.

'You see Joshua, I can't take that risk, I need this escape route should anything go wrong.'

'But what can go wrong Professor – you're just talking on TV?'

'I know, you're right, of course. But I may offend some very powerful people – I just don't know. What you need to do is have the barge ready to sail on Saturday night at about nine o'clock in the evening. I've already told my wife that it's a holiday break – so as not to alarm her you understand, and I suggest you say the same thing to Rosie. My wife will arrive with our luggage late Saturday afternoon and I should get here around nine o'clock or sooner I hope. I'll probably be on my bicycle.'

'Of course – we'll be ready. We're full with diesel, so no worries there.'

'Splendid. Oh, there's one more thing – it's probably not a good idea to tell Rosie that I'm going to be on TV on Saturday evening – just in case.'

'But does your wife know? Surly she'll want to watch?' Rosie's father asked.

'She does know, but I've told her it's in a couple of weeks, not this Saturday – if she knew she would only become over-anxious – my wife has a rather dark view of the world. The main thing to remember is that no one watches TV on Saturday evening.'

'Well, you know Rosie, Professor, ever since you gave her that laptop she hasn't any time for the TV. She did try watching, but stopped – you know why?'

'Why?' the Professor asked curiously.

'Because, she said, it bullied her own ideas.'

'She's remarkable!' the Professor exclaimed shaking his head, and he quickly continued, 'Now, I'll be in touch before Saturday, just to check everything is prepared, so keep the mobile I gave you charged.'

'You've nothing to worry about Professor, we'll be ready, and anyway, I'll see you in the operating theatre before Saturday.'

'I'm afraid not Joshua. The patient Mrs. Mills died this morning – cardiac problems apparently. So keep your mobile close.'

The two men parted. As Rosie's father returned to the barge he was trying to remember the instructions the Professor had given him, some weeks ago, about how to start the diesel motor. However, going through the Professor's mind, as he returned home, were some of the questions he wanted to ask Mr. Martin.

*

The next morning Professor Marshal finished his coffee and picked up his home phone before setting off for the hospital and called George Martin.

'Mr. Martin?'

'Professor! Great to hear from you. So tell me the good news.' Mr. Martin said cheerfully.

'The good news is I would like to appear on your programme, but first I'd like some clarification about how your programme is edited.'

'Of course, what would you like to know?'

'Your programme is live?'

'Absolutely.'

'And it is completely uncensored?'

'Of course – except if someone uses a swear word then we have by law to bleep it out.'

'That's fine – I have no intention of letting my emotions get the better of me. Now, I want to use some video material over which I have sole control, is that possible?'

'I can't see why not. How would you use it?' Mr. Martin asked hesitantly.

'Well a moment might arise in the debate in which it was relevant and I would want to be free to use it to support my case.'

'Hummm...I can't see anyone objecting to that.'

'Good. So, Mr. Martin, what must I do before Saturday?'

'Please, call me George – what must you do? Learn how to turn the world upside down in 40 minutes – my programme is trying to re-invent controversy, so the more outrageously rational you can be the more we'll support you.'

'You may, Mr. Martin – I mean George – live to regret those words.'

'That's fine! We'll see you Saturday. We'll pick you up at 7pm from the hospital. We go live at 8pm on the dot.'

*

'Good evening Ladies and Gentlemen! Welcome to tonight's Action Debates show. Tonight I have two distinguished guests who have promised us a fiery exchange of views.....My guest to my right is none other than the new Grand Muftin, Ayatollah Hussein-McDonald The Third. He's a distinguished theologian and was recently promoted to the head of the Blue Dog Temple. His aim, he told me, is to create a new, modern morality for a modern society. My guest to my left is Professor Henry Marshal, a distinguished neurosurgeon and scientist, whose recent documentary 'Into the Unknown' has won numerous awards for its vivid descriptions of neurosurgery and for its candid portrayal of surgery as an art as well as a science. Professor Marshal's aim, he told me, is to alleviate human suffering through an open-minded morality based on scientific discovery – especially in medicine. Gentlemen, welcome to the show. Ayatollah Hussein-McDonald can I start with you – is science God's curse or God's gift to Mankind?'

'First, George, let me thank you for inviting me onto the show – it's a great privilege. Is science God's gift or curse? Well, it is both, because science belongs only to God and his Prophet – comfort be upon him – science is only a gift or a curse because of what man does with it. But science itself does not belong to man. Chaothicism embodies the struggle between the Order of God's Science and the Chaos of God's Science. For example, there is a diffusion of the god-head into reality that achieves a sublime equilibrium between such things as geometry and religiosity, between mitosis and morality.'

'I see. Professor Marshal would you like to comment?'

'Yes, I would. Like many deeply religious people the Ayatollah seems lost inside a rhetoric of his own making. He builds a jungle of words inside which only he feels comfortable. First, let's be clear, science does belong to people, and it always has belonged to people. Science does not belong to some ancient, prehistoric shadow that lurks inside our minds called 'god'. It is the idea of 'god' that is a curse, not science. For thousands of years we have allowed ourselves to become enslaved by a single idea – and I'm afraid the Ayatollah is still just rattling our chains.'

'Ayatollah – are you rattling our chains?' Mr. Martin asked.

'That is a beautiful metaphor, but like so many metaphors it is false. It is false because it sees the world through only one pair of spectacles.

God's appointed Prophet – comfort be upon him – revealed God's truth through a different pair of spectacles. These spectacles have shown us that there can be such things as an ethical catalysis between a zygote and prayer, between the miracle of conception and the coming into being of the soul. These conceptions don't enslave us, on the contrary, they liberate us.'

'Professor Marshal?'

'Unfortunately I can see no freedom in the Ayatollah's words. He mixes the vocabulary of science together with the most fuzzy notions of theology, to create the impression of some profound mysticism that only he is privy to, that only he, and people like him, understand. It is obfuscation for the sole purpose of mind control, and that is why belief in a supernatural being – for which, by the way, there is not a shred of evidence – is fundamentally enslavement and not freedom.'

'Ayatollah? Are you controlling our minds?' Mr. Martin echoed.

'Of course not George. Professor Marshal seems to think that religion has some secret plan, that religion is a curse, but let me ask him to explain why the Churches, the Temples and other places of worship around the world, are doing so much good, why are they bringing comfort to the poor, health-care to the sick, education to the illiterate, shelter to the homeless. Why are we doing all this if, as Professor Marshal thinks, we only want to enslave people?'

'It's a fair point Professor?' Mr. Martin asked.

'I admit it is mostly done from a sincere wish to help – that can't be denied,' the Professor responded and he continued, 'But there is another agenda and the Ayatollah knows full well what that is. It is to increase the number of converts to their particular religion. If it was solely a desire to help and nothing more, then why don't all the different religious groups pool their stretched resources and help the needy that way? It would be far more effective? But they don't. Instead they compete like spiritual capitalists to convert as many poor people as possible to their brand of God. Help and charity is the disguise they use to proselytise desperately poor people, and it's shameful.'

'Are you ashamed Ayatollah?'

'Of course not. What the Professor has described is a gross misrepresentation of our work – and, if I may say so, quite insulting to the many thousands of selfless people around the world who have devoted their lives to helping the under-privileged. The Temple of the Blue Dog has teams of doctors working day and night assisting those in need. We – '

'You mean like your organ transplant business?' Professor Marshal cut in, 'It must earn you a tidy sum?'

'It's a valid point Ayatollah,' Mr. Martin said, but for the sake of fair-play he added, 'Maybe you'd like to clarify your position to our viewers?'

'Of course George, I'd be delighted. It's very simple – there is a terrible global shortage of transplant organs and often poor people are left to die, either because they can't afford the cost of an operation, or there is just no hospital where they live. Flying organs, of every description, in specially cooled containers to hospitals all over the world, is very costly. With some countries we have arrangements with their governments, with others we cover the costs.'

'Would someone called Dr. Abdulla-Smith be one of your suppliers of organs?' Professor Marshal asked.

'Er yes, he is. He's one of our most trusted suppliers here in the City.'

'Because,' the Professor had thrown the bait and he didn't want to lose his chance, 'there is a suggestion that your world-wide distribution of transplant organs is not so altruistic as it seems.'

'Professor Marshal,' Mr. Martin intervened, 'I think it's only fair that you explain what you mean so that the Ayatollah has a chance to defend himself.'

'Indeed I would very much like to know what the Professor is implying.' the Ayatollah said indignantly.

'I'd be glad to explain. You say you transport organs around the world to help those who are sick? Is that not so?' the Professor began reeling in his fish.

'Of course – what other reason could there be?' the Ayatollah asked with surprise.

'Ayatollah, I'd like you watch this brief video clip of Dr Abdulla-Smith – who you have just agreed is one of your most trusted suppliers of organs. He is talking with his assistant Jones who has just raised doubts about sending organs infected with MRSA overseas. However, I have to warn you, you may find the end disturbing.'

'God has given me a strong stomach Professor, please proceed.'

The Professor took from his pocket a remote and pointed it at a small TV screen on stage. What the Ayatollah and viewers saw and heard was the following -

'Yes Jones that's possible, 'one day',' the good Doctor replied with a hint of irritation in his voice, and he continued, 'but that's already been taken care of. If 'one day' we get an enquiry from some overseas government or some such, we can always blame the bad management, or the poor record-keeping, or the lame computer

skills of clerical staff in the hospitals we do business with. For all the investigators would ever know we accepted the cadavers in good faith believing them to be free of infection.'

'Hummm...'

'You seem doubtful Jones?'

'But it would not be too difficult for an investigator to see a pattern in the infection.'

'What do you mean? What 'pattern'?'

'Well, I've noticed that all those organs which we definitely know to be infected with MRSA – are somehow sent to those countries overseas, that have rejected, indeed have outlawed, Blue Dog Chaothicism. We could be accused of deliberately spreading disease to countries we have declared as Blasphemous States.'

'Are you saying Jones there is some global conspiracy theory going on here and that its epicentre is right here in this room?'

'It is feasible Sir.'

The good Doctor opened a drawer in his desk and took out a small revolver. He pointed it at Jones and said,

'You're right Jones, it is feasible. But at least your organs won't be infected,' and he fired a single shot that killed Jones outright.

'So, Ayatollah,' Professor Marshal finished, 'you see, your motives may appear altruistic but there is another, far more grotesque, far more sinister agenda to what you are doing – biological religious warfare.'

'These are grave allegations Professor,' the Ayatollah mumbled.

'No Ayatollah, they are not allegations, this is hard evidence. It is proof of an agenda within your Blue Dog Temple to export infectious disease for religious reasons. Again, it's shameful.'

'Rest assured Professor Marshal, I will personally launch an investigation into the matter and I hope the police will immediately apprehend Dr. Abdullah-Smith for this cold-blooded crime.'

George Martin felt he was losing control of which way the debate was going so he tried gently to reassert his authority and said,

'Professor Marshal this is astonishing and potentially devastating news. Never before on this show have we witnessed a real act of murder. However, I want to steer the debate away from these shocking revelations, back to the main topic and that is the centrality of religious belief in a modern society – does it have any role to play? It is clearly true that what we have just witnessed is a big setback for the Ayatollah, so, for the sake of fairness and balance, I would like to offer the Ayatollah the opportunity now, to explain his view of The Temple's role in a modern society. Ayatollah.'

'Thank you George. As probably all your viewers are aware, over the last few decades Blue Dog Chaothicism has become the fastest growing religion the world has ever seen, with thousands converting each day. And why? you may ask. I feel the answer is to be found in the way modern societies develop. First there is a period of prosperity, but this inexorably gives way to perverse, disorientated behaviour, where evil flourishes and Satan roams the streets. Men see the flesh of women and the women turn lustful because they are allowed to dress like whores. Gangs of children – some as young as eight years old – intimidate and attack old men who could be their grandfathers. Society's moral compass is being turned the wrong way by Satan's minions. We in the Blue Dog Church aim to restore dignity and respect into people's lives. We insist on making 'honour and pride' the foundation stone of the moral order – not hedonistic violence and abandon.'

'Professor Marshal would you like to comment?' Mr. Martin offered.

'Yes. The problem Ayatollah, is that of the six or seven major religions that have dominated people's lives through the centuries, each one has had its own, special, 'moral compass' – so which is the right one? The truth is no one knows – because there isn't one. And don't forget, the major religions have had over two thousand years to get their moral compasses all pointing in the same direction – but in every case they've monumentally screwed up. What is true is that each of these moral compasses has been at war with one another for most of their history – the followers of one book of good rules slaughtering the followers of another book of good rules. How many must have perished with the name of their god on their lips – it's – '

'Who with hindsight,' the Ayatollah cut in, 'has not made mistakes Professor? But to do what you're doing, to right off an entire canon of belief because of events that happened centuries ago, is like holding a candle in the darkness and fearing the dark rather than rejoicing at the light.'

'But it is science that gives the light, not a belief in the supernatural,' the Professor responded, 'It is religion that needs to celebrate the darkness, because without the darkness you would not be able to frighten everybody with make-believe demons like Satan, the AntiDog, the Devs, the Angel of Death – the list is endless. You talked a moment ago Ayatollah, about the perversity of modern society and the 'honour and pride' that Blue Dog Chaothicism wants to restore?'

'Yes.'

'Does the 'honour and pride' also include this – '

The Prof quickly pointed the remote he was still holding at the TV and there appeared on the screen a semi-clothed man astride the fully naked body of a dead girl. The semi-naked man was rhythmically moving and moaning and it was clear he was performing the sex act on a corpse. What made it especially shocking is that the Professor froze the picture showing a close up of the face of the half-naked man – it was the Grand Mufftin himself! The Grand Mufftin slowly rose threateningly out of his chair.

'How dare you! How dare you betray and besmirch the memory of this young woman! You have intruded – actually spied – on a mystic purification ceremony!'

'I beg your pardon Ayatollah but you are violating a dead girl – there's nothing mystic or pure about that, it's a despicable abomination and it's criminal.'

'Actually Professor you're wrong. It is not violation. Ritual purification – as it's properly called – was decriminalised under Purification Ordinance 23a two years ago.'

'Wait a minute. You mean to say what you are shown doing to this dead girl, on this video, is now *legal*!?'

'Absolutely. The purification statutes were put in place to protect the dead from the spiritual vicissitudes of mortality. Everyone, when they die, are actually haunted by an evil force. As priests we are now empowered to exorcise, to banish this spirit of destruction by placing our life-giving fluids into the deceased. God has spoken through the Prophet – comfort be upon him – of the need to connect with those who are making the transition between life and death. As they journey into the after-life it is our duty to protect their souls. We are engaged in enhancing the super-sensual truth of immortality.'

'No! No you're not! You're raping the dead!' the Professor exclaimed.

'Professor, belief must always transcend such banality,' the Ayatollah responded.

'Banality!? Your beliefs are worse than banal, they are morbid, perverse and based on nothing more profound than the profit motive and sexual gratification! In almost every country on Earth this sort of necrophilia is outlawed!'

'But who does it hurt Professor? No one – the dead are beyond pain,' the Ayatollah reasoned.

'But there's no...no respect!' objected Professor Marshal.

'On the contrary Professor, it is the most respectful thing one can do to those passing over – to imbue them with the divine essence of life itself, to assist their soul's journey through the darkness to the sanctity beyond death. Would you deny them that?'

'Let me make this clear in my own head Ayatollah, you and your Blue Dog priests, want people to sexually embrace the dead?'

'That's one way of putting it.'

'Well then, who should I invite to copulate with my dead mother? You perhaps? Or the man next door? Can anyone just turn up to my front door and say 'Hi, can I come in? I'd like to screw your dead wife.' ?'

'No, of course not anyone – only those ordained into the priesthood are allowed to perform the rituals of purification – that is quite clear in Ordinance 23a. And don't forget Professor, for those people who have died because they were infected with disease and such things as MRSA, the antibiotics of medicine have failed. What we in the Church are providing are spiritual antibiotics, transubstantiated hormones and medicines that have been blessed by the Prophet – comfort be upon him. The epidemiology of evil, Professor, is extensive and we would be negligent if we did not extend our protection to the dead.'

'Seldom, Ayatollah, have I heard such robust, sinister nonsense spoken to support such sinister depravity. It's like all that we hold dear and civilised is being used by psychopaths, who have become crazed by a madness so barbaric it defies description. I sincerely hope that what you are proposing is rejected by every rational being in the universe.'

'At this juncture, gentlemen, I think we should call this debate to an end – my producer is screaming into my ear-piece to get you both off the air, and I can almost feel the Earth moving beneath my feet as I speak. I apologise to any viewers who may have been offended or upset by the content of tonight's show. But as they say 'controversy is controversial'. So, are we mature enough to deal with the consequences? Time will tell. Ladies and gentlemen, thank you for watching. Goodnight.'

*

As Professor Marshal got into the studio car to take him back to St. Mary's that evening, he had no idea what the consequences of his revelations concerning the Blue Dog Church would be. His only thoughts were that he had done his duty in telling the truth. The Professor felt it was only our ability to face up to the uncompromising truth, that kept mankind from falling back into barbarism. It was truth that powered reason and reason that powered truth.

The first sign that this was not going to happen, not tonight anyway, was when the studio car turned into the road leading to the hospital. A small crowd had gathered near the main entrance and their mood was ugly. The driver asked the Professor what he should do.

'Drive on as though we're just passing – don't stop.' the Professor replied. He gave the driver directions to his house which was another thirty minutes away by car. However, when they entered the Professor's road, they noticed that, here too, were a lot of agitated people milling around in the darkness just outside the Professor's house. He told the driver to turn the car around. But this caught the attention of some of the shadowy figures and immediately a large brick slammed into the side of the car. Fortunately the driver remained calm and a second later they had sped out of harm's way back onto the main road.

After driving down several streets the Professor asked the driver to stop and let him out. He felt it was unfair to keep on asking the driver to put himself and his car at risk – and besides, he was on familiar ground, and there was, he knew in the next street, a footpath that led to the canal. He thanked the driver and said he was going to a friend's house nearby. Once the car had disappeared into the night, the Professor walked to the adjoining street, found the path and was soon walking quickly down the unlit tow-path beside the canal. He glanced at his watch but it was too dark to tell the time. He only hoped Joshua was ready to leave and had some lights on in the barge – otherwise, if he wasn't careful, he might just walk passed the barge or fall into the canal! But the pitch darkness can play strange tricks on even the most rational of minds and the Professor was no exception. Several times he saw gangs of men coming out of the blackness in front of him. But somehow they never seemed to arrive. Once he saw the tow-path disappear into the canal and he was sure he was about to plunge head first into the soupy blackness of the canal waters.

Fortunately none of these things happened. Anticipating the problem the Professor might face in the darkness, Rosie's father had indeed switched on many of the deck lights and, after walking cautiously for about half an hour, Professor Marshal felt a huge sense of relief when caught sight of the barge's lights twinkling in the distance.

'Hello!' the Professor called out as he stepped onto the barge. The cabin door opened and he was greeted with the lovely smell of an Indian curry and the smiling faces of his wife Valery, Rosie and Joshua. Never did he feel so glad to be with friends in familiar surroundings. Ten minutes later Joshua released the barge from its moorings and pushed the nose out away from the side of the canal. The Professor gently opened the throttle of the diesel motor and the barge chugged slowly and majestically into the uncertain night.

*

Travelling by night along an unlit canal is extremely hazardous. The Professor knew this from experience, but some instinct told him he had to put as much distance between himself and the city by daybreak. He therefore switched on two headlights on the bow of the barge to help him navigate through the narrow, dark corridor of water before him. For six or seven hours he chugged doggedly southwards through the darkness. All the adults and Rosie had, long ago, gone to bed and were still fast asleep when the first open fields beyond the city appeared and dawn began to lighten the eastern skies. The Professor turned the motor off and brought the barge to a gradual halt beside the canal. He jumped onto the embankment and tied a line to a tree. Then he made both aft and forward secure and decided it was time to sleep. He went down into the cabin and locked the main door behind him. Tiptoeing to his cabin he was startled to find Valery sitting up in bed watching something on her i-pad. She was clearly having one of her sleepless nights and her face certainly did not look happy. She glanced at the Professor as he entered and said with a voice full of fear,

'Henry there've been riots. Last night, in all the major cities, it seems Blue Dog fanatics have been rampaging through the streets smashing shop windows and setting churches and even hospitals on fire. The world's gone mad Henry.'

'Was it ever sane Valery?' the Professor answered hardly able to keep his eyes open.

'They say it has something to do with a TV programme that was apparently critical of the Blue Dog Temple,' Valery continued without looking away from the screen.

'Yes,...yes that was... me.' the Professor uttered as he fell fast asleep.

But Valery was too immersed in reading the reports of what had happened, to pay any attention to the mumblings of her sleep-deprived husband. However, after another few minutes she too – at long last – began to feel tired, so she turned her i-pad off and decided to join her husband and try to get a couple of hours sleep before the rest of the world woke up.

*

It was breakfast time and Auntie Jane was opening the post.

'Ah Susan, Dr. Phillips wants to see Ellie for her check-up.'

'When?'

'He's given us an appointment for tomorrow at 11am.'

'Where's his surgery?' Sam asked as she buttered some toast.

'Dimchester,' Auntie Jane replied. Susan sat at the table with Ellie on her lap. She was feeding her some toast soaked in warm milk – one of Elli's favourites.

'Dimchester? But that's miles away.' Susan commented.

'And we're not allowed to drive.' Sam added.

'That's not a problem,' Auntie Jane replied and she went on, 'I often go in to Dimchester for supplies. I borrow my neighbour's horse and trap and I go cross country down the farm tracks – it's not a car and it's not on the roads, so the law can't touch us – and we don't have to cover ourselves until we reach the town. Besides, it's quicker cross country and much more pleasant.'

Susan and Sam had been living with Auntie Jane on the small holding now for over three months, and Ellie was the absolute joy of everyone's heart. Ellie was now almost seven months old and was crawling everywhere as though she couldn't wait to explore the world, have fun and laugh. In an odd way it was Ellie that seemed to motivate the three women to make their small farm a success. Before Ellie, Susan and Sam had arrived, Auntie Jane had just subsisted on what she grew for herself, occasionally selling anything she had left over at the Saturday market in Dimchester. Now, however, there were two extra mouths to feed and a baby bursting with life and that changed everything. When Sam had regained her ability to stand and walk – after she had rescued Ellie from the log fire incident – her recovery had been rapid, and after only a week she was able to stand in the kitchen and cook meals for Auntie Jane and Susan.

It was Monday morning and the idea of travelling on Tuesday in a horse and trap across the fields to the nearest town, made Monday seem like an inconvenience. Auntie Jane called her neighbour that evening and arranged the transport. She said the journey by car from Maidensbridge to Dimchester went miles in an almost circle and took over thirty five minutes, but cross-country by trap it took just thirty. By Monday evening everything was prepared especially the list of essential supplies like brown flour for bread, babies nappies, formula milk, etc. They had to be at the doctor's at eleven so they should leave, Auntie Jane said, by ten. After supper Susan put Ellie into her cot and tickled her under her pretty chin till she giggled. Sam scolded Susan in a friendly way saying she shouldn't get Ellie too excited as they all had to get a good night's sleep, so Susan sang Ellie a lullaby and five minutes later, like magic, Ellie was fast asleep.

Auntie Jane made them all a cocoa drink as a nightcap and the three women sat together beside the fire staring thoughtfully into the flames.

*

Rosie was the first to wake. She had a nasty cough which wasn't there the night before. The barge, she vaguely remembered, had spent most of the night chugging quietly through the dark canal waters. The rhythmic sound had eventually lulled her to sleep and so she had no idea for how long or how far they had travelled. She only knew she had woken up with a sore throat and cough but everyone else was still asleep.

Despite her cough she got up and dressed. She was aware that the noise of her coughing in the rather confined space of the cabin could easily disturb the sleeping adults, so she quietly crept out and went up on deck. The barge, it appeared, had been tied to a tree next to an empty field. It was a lovely fresh, sunny morning and Rosie decided to go for a little walk. However, she hadn't gone very far when her cough started to feel painful so she doubled back and sat on a small chair on deck and tried her best not to cough.

'Good morning Rosie!' the sleepy face of the Professor appeared in the cabin doorway.

'Hi Professor,' Rosie replied as she tried unsuccessfully to stifle another cough.

'That's a nasty cough?' the Professor said frowning.

'It started when I woke up. It's sore to swallow.'

'How do you feel?' the Professor asked but Rosie didn't answer, she just made a face and shrugged her shoulders. The Professor disappeared back down into the cabin and returned a minute later with a thermometer. He took Rosie's temperature.

'Humm...38.5 degrees is a bit too high for my liking Rosie. I want you to stay here in the warm sunshine and wrap a blanket around you.'

Rosie did as she was told but an hour later after most of the others were up and having breakfast, her temperature had climbed to 39.5 and she herself had no appetite. The Professor was becoming concerned. Her surgical head wound showed no sign of being infected and was almost completely healed – indeed Rosie's dark hair had grown back so much there was now nothing to see of her surgery. Nonetheless, the Professor didn't want to take any chances. He knew Rosie had a throat infection of some description and that she needed to see a doctor who could, if needed, write a prescription for some standard antibiotics.

The Professor and Rosie's father looked at the map and saw, not far from where they were moored, a small town called Dimchester – not 30 minutes from their present position. The map showed the canal running right alongside the town and it looked like it had a mooring station for several barges. A quick internet search showed there was a Dr. Phillips in the town and the Professor used his mobile to call the surgery and arrange an appointment for 11.15am that very morning. It was already 10.05am and if they were smart they could be there by 10.40am

Rosie's father started up the diesel motor while the Professor untied the barge and pushed the nose out into the centre of the canal. A minute later they were underway towards Dimchester. Rosie still sat in her chair wrapped in a thick blanket while her father took the helm and the Professor stood nearby on deck studying the map.

'Round this bend there should be a narrow bridge over the canal,' the Professor commented to Rosie's father. And sure enough, hardly had they begun to turn into the bend than the bridge came into view. But just as the front of the barge began to slide under the bridge, a horse trotted over the bridge pulling a small buggy with three women. The women all spontaneously waved to those on the barge and the Professor and Rosie waved back and they were gone.

Thirty minutes later they docked at Dimchester. They had about half an hour to find the doctor's surgery. However, in a town as small as Dimchester, that was going to be easy.

*

It was 11.10 am and Susan, wearing her full durka and jiba, was sitting in the waiting room of Dr. Phillips's surgery, with Ellie

157

squirming on her lap. Ellie obviously didn't like being so constrained – especially as she too had to wear a tiny jiba covering her face. She kept repeatedly pulling it off but the stern looks from the doctor's receptionist told Susan to put it back on.

The door to the surgery waiting room opened and Rosie and her father entered. Rosie's father told the receptionist that Rosie had an appointment for 11.15am but the annoyed receptionist told him to take a seat and wait because the doctor was running late due to a former emergency.

The waiting room was quite small and carpeted. There were two rows of chairs along opposite walls so that when Rosie's father sat down he was directly opposite Susan and Ellie. They were the only patients waiting to see the doctor. After a few minutes Rosie whispered to her father that the baby opposite them was 'cute'. Rosie's father just smiled. Ellie, however, was proving to be a handful and she squirmed and wriggled until Susan let her slide gently to the floor. Immediately Ellie pulled off her jiba and started to crawl across the small, carpeted space towards Rosie. When she reached Rosie she put out her hand and pulled Rosie's sock. Rosie giggled and said,

'Hello, what's your name?' Ellie responded with a gurgle sound and a sweet smile. Rosie's father glanced and smiled at Susan who was watching Ellie carefully, and said in a friendly way,

'She's quite a charmer.'

'No talking between the sexes!' snapped the receptionist who pointed to the large sign pinned to the noticeboard. It instructed patients that only women who were accompanied by a male relative such as a father, brother, uncle or cousin, could be spoken to by an unrelated male.

Susan shrugged her shoulders and Rosie's father looked down at Ellie who was still playing with Rosie's socks.

'You're tickling me!' Rosie laughed and she stroked Ellie's blonde curls. Susan stood up and reached across to pick up the playful Ellie. As she did so Rosie noticed something – a piece of jewellery – fell down around Susan's wrist. Rosie looked at it for the briefest of seconds and then Susan sat back with Ellie again wriggling on her lap. For a minute Rosie became very thoughtful. Then she leant up and whispered into her father's ear –

'Dad! That woman's wearing one of your bracelets!'

Rosie's father glanced at Rosie and frowned. He looked across at Susan but he could only see the tips of her fingers as she vainly struggled to stop Ellie from getting down a second time. Beneath the woman's full durka and jiba he could see nothing. Susan had put Ellie's jiba back on and Ellie had promptly pulled it off again and this time she threw it to the floor. As Susan reached down to retrieve it, Rosie and her father watched. Sliding down Susan's arm a bracelet stopped at Susan's wrist. Instantly Rosie's father recognised it as the bracelet he had made for his wife over a year ago. What was it doing on this strange woman? He stood up and pointed. But just at this moment the receptionist called out to Susan –

'Young woman! You can go in now! The doctor will see you!'

'That...' Rosie's father tried to say as Susan walked passed him with Ellie in her arms.

'No communication is allowed Mr. Harrison!! Please sit down!' the receptionist shouted.

Rosie and her father took their seats again and glanced at each other.

'It's your mother's bracelet! I'm certain.' Rosie's father said in a low, passionate voice. As they waited all kinds of questions and implausible answers came and went in Rosie's father's head. He just had to find out where this woman had found it – but how if he wasn't allowed to talk to her? Ten minutes later he was still trying to think of what to do when he heard the doctor open his office door -

'She's doing fine! Just bring Ellie back in five months and we'll do her first one year check-up. Goodbye!'

'Mr. Harrison! You may go in now!' ordered the receptionist. As Susan walked towards the door, the doctor came into the waiting area, shook Mr. Harrison's hand and ushered him and Rosie into his office. 'Ellie! Ellie! The baby's name!' was all Rosie's father could think and it took a huge effort for him to concentrate on why he was there. He explained about Rosie's sore throat and cough which had started earlier that morning. Dr. Phillips examined Rosie's tongue and throat and took her temperature. He said there was nothing to worry about because it looked like a typical childhood throat infection. He recommended Rosie stay in bed for a couple of days and if her temperature did not start to come down and the coughing symptoms continued, to give her a course of antibiotics for which he wrote a prescription. Ten minutes later they said goodbye and Rosie and her father went out onto the street. Now they had to find the pharmacy.

However, Rosie's father also wanted desperately to find the woman and Ellie and he scanned up and down the street, but they had vanished. Further down the main street he saw the sign of a pharmacist so he and Rosie headed in that direction. As they passed by the various shops his eyes searched and searched for the woman and the child Ellie, but in vain. They reached the pharmacy and went in.

At that very moment Susan, with Ellie in her arms, walked out of the supermarket right next door to the pharmacy and as she passed the automatic doors to the pharmacy Ellie again pulled off her jiba and threw it down. The automatic doors hissed open as the jiba fell onto the doormat just inside. Susan took one quick step into the pharmacy doorway and picked up Ellie's jiba. Some instinct made Rosie glance over her shoulder and she saw Ellie waving at her. Immediately Rosie pulled her dad's arm. Susan, who hadn't noticed Rosie or her father, turned and left. Rosie's father grabbed the medicine the pharmacist was offering him and ran out into the street.

'Excuse me!' he called, but Susan kept on walking. 'She probably thinks I'm an entrapment agent,' Rosie's father thought but he couldn't just let her walk away. He tried again. He ran a little closer behind Susan and called out,

'That bracelet around your wrist! I gave it to my wife two years ago! I made it! Please! Where did you find it!?

Susan kept walking, but gradually her steps became slower. Eventually, still with her back to Rosie's father, she stopped. Ellie looked over Susan's shoulder at Rosie and her father and smiled.

THE END.